# Dream of a Falling Eagle

## A MONGO MYSTERY

by GEORGE C. CHESBRO

SIMON & SCHUSTER

SIMON & SCHUSTER
Rockefeller Center
1230 Avenue of the Americas
New York, NY 10020

SIMON & SCHUSTER and colophon are registered trademarks of
Simon & Schuster Inc.

Designed by Hyun Joo Kim
Manufactured in the United States of America

1   3   5   7   9   10   8   6   4   2

Library of Congress Cataloging-in-Publication Data
Chesbro, George C.
Dream of a falling eagle : a Mongo mystery / by George C. Chesbro
p.    cm.    1. Mongo (Fictitious character)—Fiction. I. Title.
PS3553.H359D74   1996
813'.54—dc20    96-19331    CIP

ISBN 0-684-83053-1

*To Otto Penzler*

**W**e were three-quarters of the way up the long gravel
driveway leading to the torturer's house, driving
slowly to avoid a number of deep potholes, when
Garth abruptly slammed on the brakes and turned off
the headlights and ignition of his Jeep Cherokee. We never went anywhere these days without our guns, and I immediately reached for
the Beretta in my shoulder holster. "What's the matter?"

My brother put a finger to his lips and whispered, "It looks like the
general has already entertained guests this evening, and they're just
leaving."

I leaned forward in my seat and squinted as I looked out through
the windshield, but the bright lights burning on both floors of the
shabby house at the end of the driveway only made the surrounding
darkness seem more impenetrable. I tried shielding my eyes with my
hand, but it didn't help. "I don't see anything."

"At least three men. I saw them moving across that patch of moonlight on the lawn at the right side of the house, heading into the
woods. They're gone now."

"Or moving on us."

Garth drew his Colt and turned the interior light switch to off, and
then we both stepped out of the car, guns raised and sweeping the

driveway ahead of us and the woods on either side. We moved to the front of the car and stood side by side in the darkness for a few minutes, listening for the snap of a twig or rustle of gravel that might indicate we were being stalked, but there was no sound other than a shrill chorus of crickets wailing their little hearts out in the hot and humid August night. Finally I nudged Garth and we stepped to opposite sides of the driveway, walking slowly toward the house on narrow aprons of grass as we kept our guns steadily trained ahead of us. If the general's evening visitors had seen our headlights and wanted to ambush us, it seemed logical that they would have waited inside the house instead of exiting out the back, but our experiences of the past few months had made us very cautious. Of late, there were an even greater number of people than usual who wanted to facilitate the permanent retirement of the Frederickson brothers, and our current enemies of record were a lot better equipped and more organized than your average gaggle of thugs.

The front door was half open and had a dead thing nailed to it, which we knew meant we would find another dead thing inside. It didn't take us long to find it. What was left of General Vilair Michel was strapped into a straight-backed chair in a corner of his blood-painted second-floor bedroom facing out on the driveway. His severed tongue lay neatly in his lap, and dark gouts of blood were still oozing from his eye sockets, mouth, and the hole in his chest where his heart had been. We didn't bother looking around for the missing organ, because we knew we wouldn't find it. The clear plastic raincoats the killers had used to protect their clothing were crumpled in a heap at the foot of the bed.

"Christ," I mumbled, turning away. I should have been getting used to this kind of scene by now, but I still had to fight the urge to vomit.

"Actually, he's not in as bad shape as some of the other victims,"

Garth said in a flat tone. "He still has his pants on. We must have interrupted them."

I swallowed bile, took a deep breath to try to settle my stomach. The rank smell of blood and the feces that the terrified Vilair Michel had let loose before he died was overwhelming. "That was real lucky for the general."

"Let's see if our friends overlooked anything this time."

We might have interrupted the killers at their pleasure, but apparently not before they had attended to the serious side of their business, first chatting up the general before carving him up, making sure he told them what incriminating documents, if any, he had in his possession—and then they'd ransacked the place anyway, just to make sure he hadn't forgotten anything in what must have been his paralyzing and mind-shrinking fear in the face of the evil that had seeped into his home from the dark, suppurating sores in his culture. Every drawer and file cabinet in what appeared to have been his office and study had been pulled out or turned over, and papers were strewn everywhere. Using our handkerchiefs to avoid leaving fingerprints, we sifted through the debris, but could find nothing that interested us—no forged passports or other official documents, no list of names, no diary.

In the faint hope that Michel might have squirreled away something useful in another part of the house, we worked our way through the rest of the rooms and closets, inspecting drawers and cupboards and shelves, moving things around with pencils, but we found nothing of value to us. Our last stop was the basement, which was virtually bare except for an old, dilapidated washing machine and dryer, and some rough wooden shelves littered with rusting tools and spattered paint cans. There was a small area at the north end that had been partitioned off from the rest of the basement with unpainted Sheetrock with a doorway cut into it. Garth went in there and turned on a light while I halfheartedly rooted around on the shelves I could reach.

"Hey, Mongo," Garth called from the other room. "Come on in here and check this out."

I walked through the entranceway, stopped, and grunted with surprise. This area, too, was bare, except for what appeared to be a makeshift altar of sorts set up along the opposite wall. The altar was constructed from empty plastic milk crates set on their sides and draped with black velvet that had been kept free of lint and dust with careful and regular brushings. On the altar were candles of various lengths and thicknesses, crudely carved wooden fetishes, curved daggers, and hand-painted *vèvès*—voodoo symbols similar to the ones scrawled in blood on the walls of the bedroom upstairs—and a large golden cross that looked as if it had gotten lost and wandered into the wrong neighborhood.

"Well, well," I said, walking over to stand beside my brother in front of the altar. "It seems the general was a serious practitioner himself of the old mumbo-jumbo."

"Didn't do him much good, did it?"

The golden cross was in the center of the altar, at the base of a circle of *vèvès*, daggers, and red candles carefully arranged around a black-and-white photograph that, judging from the blur around the edges, had been taken from a distance with a telephoto lens. The photo was a head-and-shoulders shot of what appeared to be a light-skinned black man, most likely Haitian, like the general. The man had been caught looking directly toward the camera, as if sensing the presence of the photographer, and there was what could be described as an expression of menace on his face, although his features were not menacing in themselves. He had a longish, triangular face with a thin chin, thin lips and nose, and high, angular cheekbones. He had smooth skin, and he looked to be in his early or mid-fifties—

although his thick head of white hair suggested he might be a decade older. His eyes were his most striking feature, almost too large and round for the rest of his face, crow-black and piercing. He wore the black tunic and reversed collar of a Roman Catholic priest.

Garth continued, "Now, who do you suppose that is?"

"Good question. Whoever he is, he seems to have been pretty important to the general—center stage on his voodoo altar." I paused, glanced at my brother. "You don't suppose the Spring Valley police would give us a copy of that photograph if we asked real nice?"

Garth smiled thinly. "In your dreams. Maybe in a few weeks, sometime down the line after we've come up with some plausible explanation of how it is we happen to know about the photograph in the first place. We really don't want to answer all the questions they'll want to ask."

"We'll call this in anonymously on nine-one-one after we leave, wait until after the news hits the papers, then go in and ask for a copy after we properly introduce ourselves."

"They probably won't release information about the photograph— you know it's the kind of potential evidence and telling little detail homicide investigators like to keep to themselves. We'd have to explain how we know about it, which would mean admitting we were here at the crime scene. That could spell very big trouble. I'm operating in my own backyard here. Mary and I don't need the publicity that would be bound to come my way, and you and I don't need the distraction. We've got a tight deadline, and we're running out of time."

"Hey, when you're right, you're right," I said, leaning over slightly in the direction of the photograph and rubbing my palms together. "But that photo could prove a lot more valuable to us than to the Spring Valley PD. I don't suppose the cop in you would permit us to just take the thing?"

Garth shook his head. "I want it as much as you do, but swiping items from a crime scene just isn't a good idea. We'll recognize him if we see him."

"Okay. Let's get out of here and find a pay phone."

*"Freeze, motherfuckers! Get your hands way up in the air and turn around very slowly! Do it now!"*

"Shit," Garth muttered.

"Piss, snot, corruption, pillage, and spitting on the floor."

*"You're both a half second from dead, motherfuckers! Get those hands up in the air and turn around slowly!"*

Garth and I did as we were told and found ourselves facing two of Spring Valley's Finest, a white male and an Amazon of a black woman who was at least a foot taller than her partner. It was the woman who had spoken. They must have been wearing shoes with crepe soles, because we hadn't heard them come up behind us. Both police officers were standing just inside the entranceway to the altar area, pointing their service revolvers at us.

"Uh-oh," Garth said.

I swallowed hard, nodded to the two police officers, and flashed my most cherubic smile. "You got that right."

# CHAPTER 2

*T*he small interrogation room to which I was taken and left alone, presumably to reflect upon the error of my ways, smelled of fresh paint. Everything was a cream color— the floor, walls, ceiling, table, and two straight-backed chairs. Even the large ceramic ashtray on the table was a cream color. The monotone, cut-rate interior decoration had a slightly disorienting effect, which I supposed was its purpose. I could hear the low bass hum of air-conditioning somewhere beyond the walls, but it wasn't cooling this place; the room was hot.

I sat up straight in one of the chairs at the table, hands folded in front of me, and stared at the one-way mirror to my right, wondering how many detectives were staring back at me while somebody ran our names and licenses through the system and checked our bona fides. About forty-five minutes later a tall, slim black man with a large strawberry birthmark on his left cheek entered the room. He looked to be about thirty. He wore a nicely tailored brown summer suit with matching tie, highly polished black shoes. The name tag over his badge read "Beauvil."

The detective sat down across from me, stared at me for a few moments with his dark eyes, then said evenly, "You and your brother are in deep shit, Frederickson."

"Yes, Detective. I know."

"Your brother tells quite a story about how the two of you came to be in that house at that particular time. Let's see how yours matches up to it."

"Meaning no disrespect, Detective, but my brother hasn't told you anything but his name, rank, and serial number."

Beauvil's eyes narrowed slightly. "You seem pretty certain of that."

"My brother can be sullen, uncooperative, and even downright cranky. I'm the one with the sunny, cooperative disposition, so he always lets me do the talking in situations like this."

"Do you think this is funny?"

"No, sir. I was explaining why I was certain Garth hadn't told you anything."

"What kind of situation is this?"

"Very, very sticky."

"You've already been read your rights when you were arrested at the crime scene. You've declined legal representation, but I'm going to ask you again. You want a lawyer?"

"No."

"I suspect you do."

"You suspect wrong. Why so solicitous, Detective? Are you this polite to all your perps?"

"Who you are commands a certain amount of respect. Also, the fact that you're both so well known means that your arrest is probably going to generate a lot of national publicity. Everything's going to be done by the book. I don't want the Spring Valley PD to end up looking like the LAPD. Now, considering your reputation and all you have to lose in this matter, I would think you'd want a lawyer representing you at this interrogation."

"Thanks, Detective. I really do appreciate your concern, but you can let me worry about that."

"You had three handguns between the two of you—your brother's Colt, and your Beretta and Seecamp."

"All three duly licensed, with special carry permits."

"You don't have a license not to report a brutal crime."

"We were just about to do precisely that."

"Unfortunately for the two of you, somebody beat you to it."

"Who? If it was a man with a Creole accent, it was probably one of the killers. They're an impatient lot, and they wanted to make sure you didn't take too long to discover their handiwork."

"You know the drill, Frederickson; I'll ask the questions." He paused, leaned back slightly in his chair, and regarded me rather archly. "The two of you may be famous, but you're also a couple of cold-blooded and arrogant sons of bitches. You see a man who's been slaughtered like a pig, and then you calmly proceed to take a tour of his house, disturbing the crime scene."

"I don't know how cold-blooded and arrogant we are, but we didn't disturb any crime scene; the place had already been tossed before we got there. As for our reaction to the torture, mutilation, and murder of the victim, we've seen it before, and the man got what he deserved—not necessarily in that order."

Beauvil blinked slowly, said quietly, "You'd better explain that."

I glanced toward the mirror, addressing whoever might be looking in and listening. "Things are moving along pretty quickly here, and they could get out of hand. Again meaning no disrespect, Detective, but I'm not certain how much detail the Spring Valley Police Department really wants to know. Maybe your chief should join us, and we could go to another room that isn't quite so public."

"You'll deal with me right here and now, Frederickson!" Beauvil snapped, slapping his palm on the table for emphasis. He paused, lowered his voice to just above a whisper. "You don't seem to realize the seriousness of your situation. It's more than just 'sticky.' We're not just talking about the two of you losing your P.I. licenses. You could end up doing some very serious jail time."

I looked away from the mirror, sighed. "Detective, what I'm most worried about at the moment isn't jail time, it's getting fired."

"Are you crazy? You and your brother could be facing first-degree murder charges."

"Spare me that heat, Detective. I'm trying to have a serious conversation with you. I understand we've got problems here, but being charged with murder isn't one of them. The vic was missing a heart. You didn't find it in our pockets, and your investigators won't find it at the house. You think we ate it? Right now it's reposing in a clay jar, right beside the rum bottle that holds the victim's spirit captive. That's part of *their* drill."

The detective tensed slightly. He started to look toward the mirror, then caught himself and stared hard at me. An ashen pallor had appeared around his strawberry birthmark, and something that looked very much like surprise moved in his ebony eyes.

I continued, "You haven't been to the crime scene, have you, Detective? This interrogation is a rush job. There are symbols called *vèvès* painted all over the vic's bedroom walls, which means this was a goddamn voodoo ritual murder. That's going to create quite a stir in Spring Valley, considering the size of your Haitian population. Do Garth and I look like voodoo priests? Before you start threatening to charge my brother and me with murder, you should be thinking about just how you plan to release this information and handle the investigation. What's happened is going to be very unsettling to a lot of people in your village."

The detective controlled his reaction quickly, but not before I had seen fear film his eyes and tighten his lips. He had been visibly shaken. Considering the fact that this minor breakdown in proper interrogation technique was taking place under the eyes of others, one or more of whom might be his superiors, I felt sympathy for the man.

He'd been sent in virtually cold, with a limited briefing, and had apparently had little idea of what he was going to hear.

"You're Haitian, aren't you, Detective?"

"I said I'd ask the questions, Frederickson."

I removed two business cards from my pocket, set them down between us on the table. "Detective Beauvil," I said evenly, "I want you to do us all a favor. It will help enormously if we can carve out the parameters of this conversation we're having. The one number is the FBI field office in New York. The FBIs have grown to thoroughly despise the Fredericksons over the years; they think we're *really* arrogant sons of bitches. The feeling is mutual. But they'll tell you we're straight arrows, and that we're on the side of the angels on this one. They'll also strongly urge you to cut us some slack on this business of not immediately calling you when we walked into the crime scene."

"What the hell does the FBI have to do with this?"

"Let them tell you. You might ask for Special Agent Mackey, but you can speak to anybody there. The FBIs will be working with you *very* closely on this case, which I'm sure makes your heart sing. The other number is where you can reach our current client. She'll vouch for us and tell you what we're up to. But she's tough as nails, and she is going to fire our asses if she finds out we went traipsing through a crime scene before reporting it—which I admit we did, but we didn't disturb anything. We had good reason. So I'd appreciate it if you'd be a *bit* discreet when you explain to her what we're doing sitting here in the Spring Valley police station. She's a retired senator, and if you'll look at the card I'm sure you'll recognize her name."

The detective didn't look at the cards. "You were overheard suggesting the removal of an item from the basement of the victim's house."

"Just idle chatter. Garth and I always joke around like that."

Beauvil's eyes were cold as he abruptly reached out and brushed his arm across the table, sweeping the cards to the floor. He took a small tape recorder from the pocket of his suit jacket, set it down between us, and turned it on. "This incident took place within the village of Spring Valley, Frederickson, and we don't need the FBI or some retired senator to tell us how to do our job. If you want to make a statement, do it."

"I thought I already had."

"You haven't even begun to tell me what I want to hear. You want to keep tap dancing, we'll book the two of you and you can wait overnight in a cell for arraignment in the morning. Robert Frederickson, you've been read your rights and have waived your right to the presence of an attorney. Is that correct?"

"That's correct," I replied, leaning back in my chair and breathing another heavy sigh.

"Are you making this statement of your own free will?"

"Well, that might be stretching the—"

"Start at the beginning. Why were you at the house of the murder victim?"

"We had an appointment. He was expecting us."

"He was expecting you?"

"That's what I said."

"Judging from your pronounced lack of sorrow at his demise, I take it you weren't exactly friends. Why would he agree to see you?"

"We had the goods on him. He knew we knew he was in this country illegally, on a very expertly forged passport we dearly would have loved to get our hands on. He was afraid we could get him shipped back to Haiti, or expose his identity and past to the Haitian community here. He didn't care for either prospect, and we'd led him to think we could cut a deal. We were planning to squeeze his ass for more information."

"On behalf of this retired senator?"

"On behalf of the president of the United States."

That got his attention, and he sat up straighter. "You told me this woman was your client."

"Senator Harriet Frawley. She's the head of a Special Presidential Commission."

"Investigating what?"

"Willful malfeasance and criminal activity on the part of the Central Intelligence Agency, specifically its Operations Directorate, over the past thirty years, with an eye toward drastically overhauling—or even dismantling—the CIA, thus saving American taxpayers a minimum of three billion dollars a year and the world a lot of grief."

Beauvil stared at me, and I stared back. We sat in silence for what seemed to me a long time, but was probably only a minute or two. Finally the detective said, "Go on."

"Go on? That was my punch line. Haven't I sung enough for our supper? I explained to you what we were doing at the vic's house, and why we were poking—uh, looking—around. We're investigating something that's much bigger than this one murder. I've also assured you that we're the good guys, and we have the FBI and a retired senator who's working for the president of the United States to back us up. Garth lives here in Rockland County—in Cairn. Call Chief Bond of the Cairn PD if you want character references."

"Ah yes, Cairn," Beauvil said with more than a trace of sarcasm in his voice. "Hollywood on the Hudson, home of the rich and famous."

"Not just the rich and famous, Detective, and Cairn isn't Hollywood on the Hudson. Give me a break and spare me the local politics. I'm saying you have a local police chief to vouch for Garth and me. Garth is local. If you pursue this, *The Journal News* is going to splash it all over page one. Then *The New York Times* and the rest of the national media will pick up on the story, and soon after that Garth and I will be taken off this investigation. We wouldn't like that. This case is personal to my brother and me. But, even more important, premature publicity is not what the commission wants or needs, and the entire investigation could be compromised. Granted that it would be the Fredericksons' fault, because we displayed a serious lapse in judgment by waiting too long to call you, but if this blows up, the Spring Valley PD could take some hits too. You said you didn't want the department to look foolish."

"The Spring Valley Police Department is simply doing its job by investigating a murder. You and your brother were caught disturbing the crime scene."

"We didn't disturb any—"

"Tell me more about this commission, Frederickson. Why should the president want to dismantle the CIA?"

"I didn't say he did. *I* want him to take apart the whole damn outfit, because I don't think reorganization or other half measures will do the trick. The problems there are systemic. But dismantling is only one of several measures he—or, more likely, his successor—will have to consider. The commission's job is to gather information, submit a final report, and possibly make recommendations. May I ask if you followed the Aldrich Ames case?"

Beauvil nodded curtly.

"Ames was a worm that got loose, and as a result a whole lot of other worms started wriggling to get out of sight at the bottom of the can. He was the most destructive traitor in American history, a man responsible for the deaths of at least two dozen agents. But the real culprit is the CIA culture. Ames couldn't have held a job outside the agency selling used cars, but his superiors entrusted him with the nation's secrets and gave him life-and-death control over scores of people. Ames was a known drunk, incorrigibly irresponsible and sloppy. That was his track record over the years. So what did the CIA do with this fool? They kept promoting him. And what happened after it was discovered he was a Soviet mole? Nothing. Nobody even got demoted, much less fired, and a couple of retired officers got mildly nasty letters."

"I said I was familiar with the Ames case, Frederickson."

"The point is that the Ames incident finally tipped the scales. A lot of important people in government have been unhappy with the CIA for a long time, because the agency has been out of control for a long time. But not much could be done because the CIA and its friends were too powerful, and it was seen as necessary to counter Russia and the KGB. All this, of course, changed with the collapse of the USSR and when it was discovered that the CIA had been consistently overestimating Russian strength for decades in order to keep fattening their own budget. The Ames incident opened all this up. People who thought their Operations department—which is what that multibillion dollar circus is really all about—was staffed with a lot of James Bonds discovered it was really a Woody Allen movie. A number of congressional committees were planning to hold hearings, but the last election changed all that. The CIA has always had close ties to the right wing in this country—in fact, that's a facet of this investigation. With the right wing controlling both houses of Congress, plans for the hearings were dumped. Finally, although he denies it, the chances that this president is going to be reelected in November are none to nil. He's almost certainly going to be replaced by a conservative from the other party, and very likely it will be somebody from the hard right. That person isn't going to make any changes in the CIA. So he decided to do something about the problem while he still had the chance. He appointed his own commission to look into the company's activities over the years. Garth and I were offered a piece of the action. We're just one team of investigators among many

working on this thing. We were assigned what you might call the
'Haiti desk.' Other investigators are looking into CIA activity in Iran,
El Salvador, Chile—countries all over the globe. The final report will
be compiled, published, and made public before the election. Then,
no matter what happens, the information will be out there, and the
new president, Congress, and the American people will have to deal
with it, whether they want to or not. That's what this is all about."

Beauvil shrugged. "For you and your brother, maybe. Our concern
is with a murder investigation. What was the victim's name?"

"General Vilair Michel. He started off as a teenage Ton-ton Ma-
coute, then grew up into a big player in both Fraph and the army. For
a few years he was commandant of Fort Dimanche—Haiti's Tre-
blinka. That's where he used to do to other people what was now done
to him. In Fort Dimanche, political prisoners were raped, castrated,
blinded, and had their limbs amputated. Michel got off easy."

"You're saying you think this was a revenge killing?"

"No. I know it wasn't a revenge killing. Michel was murdered to
shut his mouth, and to put a good scare into any other Haitian who
might be tempted to cooperate with the investigation. The people
we're after are plugged in everywhere. Somehow they found out—or
guessed—that Michel would be willing to talk to us. So they made
sure they talked to him first. There have been five ritual killings just
like this one—all Haitians, each person a potential witness to illegal
CIA activity in Haiti. Two of the murders occurred in New Orleans,
one in California, and two in New York. That's why you're going to
have FBIs in your pants five minutes after you finish talking to them.
It's also why I suspect it was one of the killers who called you. They
want the publicity; they want to terrify Haitians. The good news is
that all of the victims were murderous thugs like Michel; they're the
only people who know what really went on in Haiti."

Beauvil frowned slightly. The film of fear had returned to his dark eyes. He might be an educated man living in the United States, but he was still obviously made decidedly uncomfortable by talk about voodoo and ritual murders. "What really did go on in Haiti?" he asked quietly. "How is the CIA connected?"

"Jesus Christ," I said, rolling my eyes toward the ceiling. "Let me count the ways. Let's see if I can't just sketch in the big picture. You ever catch a TV program back in the sixties called *The Prisoner?* Patrick McGoohan?"

"No," the detective replied curtly. "My family didn't have a television set. They couldn't afford it."

"It was about a top British Intelligence agent who quits the service in a huff. Because he knows too many secrets and is considered untrustworthy, he's drugged and bundled off to an island that's essentially a prison. That premise could have been modeled on Haiti—or so Garth and I have good reason to believe. Right now I'm betting the CIA wishes they had shipped Aldrich Ames off to Haiti a long time ago. But then, they never considered Ames untrustworthy. This case does have its humorous side."

"You're saying the CIA used Haiti as a penal colony?"

"Depending on who was sent there and for what reason, it was used as a penal colony, a death camp at Fort Dimanche, or luxury resort among the villas up in the hills. The problem is that all this is very difficult to prove. Former Haitian army officers who could provide hard evidence keep getting their hearts cut out. What we can prove is that Vilair Michel, along with hundreds—possibly thousands—of Ton-ton Macoutes, Fraph people, army officers, and government officials, was on the CIA payroll. CIA money has been going into Haiti for years, going all the way back to Papa Doc—who was probably a CIA creation. We think we've collected enough evidence to convince reasonable people that the whole country of Haiti served as a kind of offshore bank for the CIA, which used it to hide and launder large amounts of money generated through things like drug running, and which it then used to finance other secret, illegal operations. Needless to say, there was no congressional oversight of these affairs. That fool William Casey dreamed of setting up what he called an 'off-the-shelf' operation. What he didn't know was that people buried deep within the organization had already created precisely such a thing decades before, and it was running smoothly. Casey's another guy I'll bet the CIA wishes it had shipped off to Haiti. They probably killed him."

The corners of the detective's mouth curled upward in just the slightest trace of a smile. "With the CIA's infamous brain-tumor pill?"

"Ah. A flash of humor there. I take that as a good sign."

"That would be a mistake."

"Try to remember that paranoids often do have real enemies."

"What about Oliver North?"

"Just a tool. North is a CIA poster boy—the kind of person the company loves to have around to run errands, and run for office. What Garth and I are trying to prove, Detective, is that that whole goddamn hellhole of a country was essentially a CIA asset. It was a company store, if you will, owned lock, stock, and barrel by the CIA. Aristide's election can be viewed as a hostile takeover. They did what they could to stop it, and gave it their best shot with the military junta, but they came up short. Now we're trying to get hold of the books of that company store. That isn't easy, since most records over there were literally just jotted notes on pieces of paper. It also isn't so easy interviewing the major shopkeepers when they keep winding up dead. And *that*, Detective, is why Garth and I were doing a walkabout in the good general's home."

"Jesus," Beauvil said in a flat tone.

"None of this need concern you, Detective; as you've pointed out, your responsibility is to investigate a murder that took place in the village of Spring Valley. But that killing is just a small part of a very large conspiracy that Garth and I are digging into. We would have called you, and then we'd have called the FBI ourselves. If you cut us loose and let us continue our work, there's at least a chance that the men who did this, as well as the bigger fish who put together and run this voodoo hit squad, will be caught and brought to justice. Bring us down, cause a stir in the newspapers that could end our role in the overall investigation by the commission, and your chances for ever catching them are diminished. A great deal of work by many people could be put in jeopardy by the premature disclosure of what we've been up to these past months. It's up to you."

The detective's hand trembled ever so slightly as he reached out to turn off the tape recorder. His eyes gleamed, and his neck was slightly flushed. He seemed about to say something when there was a single, sharp rap from the other side of the one-way mirror. Beauvil pocketed the tape recorder, then stood up. He stooped to pick up the cards he had swept to the floor, then walked briskly out of the room, closing the door behind him.

Twenty minutes passed, time I spent with my feet flat on the floor, hands folded on the table, staring at the opposite wall and trying not to look as anxious as I felt. Then I heard the door open, and I turned to find my brother standing in the doorway. His soulful brown eyes glinted with amusement, and there was a thin, wry smile on his face. He said quietly, "It looks like you've done it again, you silver-tongued devil."

"We're outta here?"

"Yeah. Let's get a move on before they change their minds."

"Right," I said, rising and walking quickly through the door Garth held open for me.

We headed down a narrow corridor, past two other interrogation

rooms and a holding cell. As we turned a corner and entered the
booking area I could see into a small office where Beauvil was standing and talking to a portly, gray-haired man wearing a chief's uniform
and sitting behind a littered desk. The two officers who had arrested
us were standing across the lobby, staring at us with curiosity. We
nodded to them, then headed for the exit.

"Hold it!"

We stopped just before the exit doors, turned to see Beauvil, who
had just come out of the office. Behind him, the chief was closing the
blinds covering his window. Beauvil came up to us and ushered us
outside.

"We're doing you two a favor because we don't want to interfere
with the work of any Presidential Commission," he said softly,
squinting into the rising sun. "Now you do us one."

"Name it," I replied.

"We don't want to be accused of showing any favoritism toward our
local celebrity here and his famous brother. We don't want any of this
to come back and bite us in the ass."

"That's not going to happen, Detective."

"The easiest way to handle this is not to file a report that the two
of you were arrested at a crime scene shortly after a man was murdered. As far as we're concerned, you weren't there—and you
haven't been here."

"Garth and I hardly ever come to Spring Valley, and we don't even
know where the police station is."

"The report will state that an anonymous caller phoned in about
the killing on nine-one-one. The caller also advised us to notify the
FBI."

"That's exactly the way it would have happened."

"The FBIs will figure it was you and get in touch."

"Or we'll call them when we get back to the city. Thanks, Detective." I paused, scratched my head. "Uh, there is one other little thing. When we were busted we were looking at a photograph placed on a voodoo altar down in Michel's basement. It could be important. Is there any way—"

"No, there isn't," the detective replied curtly. "You've obviously been working with the FBI. Get a copy from them."

"You ever have occasion to work with the FBIs, Detective? If not, you're in for a very unpleasant education. They have the best crime labs and data bank in the world, but they must screen their field agents for a genetic predisposition to hating to share evidence or information. They're also hostile to private investigators in general, and us in particular, even though we're supposed to be working together."

"I can't help you," Beauvil said before abruptly turning and heading back into the station house.

# CHAPTER 3

lthough Garth and I had good reason to believe that everything I had told the Spring Valley police detective about the CIA's links to Haiti was gospel truth, the fact of the matter was that our hard evidence was even flimsier than I had indicated. Others, including a good number of the reasonable people who were our target audience, might fairly label the tale as being based on nothing more than rumor, gossip, and innuendo. That was the bad news. The good news was that our task was simply to prepare a report, not bring absolute proof into a court of law. We had enough evidence to mark out the beginning of a trail leading into a very dark swamp where poisonous things grew. The brutal, voodoo torture-murders of six of our potential key informers spoke for themselves. We would point the way, and then it would be up to congressional committees with subpoena powers to decide how deeply they wanted to wade into the Haitian nightmare. We were also dead certain that, for years, the CIA had been funneling its secret funds in Haiti to various right-wing organizations in the United States through a complex chain of dummy corporations that resembled a Tower of Babel. After months of work, we'd only begun to unravel that rotten skein, so the circumstantial evidence we did have would go into a separate appendix of our report, along with the rest of the rumors, gossip, and innuendo, which we'd call Suggestions for Further Inquiry.

Time does fly when you're having fun, and our time was just about up. Our report was due by the end of the month, in three weeks, so we were essentially done with our investigating. Now we had to collate the data we had compiled and shape it into usable form, then rev up the word processor and actually write the report. The document would be lengthy and, we hoped, a real attention-grabber. It was going to be a lot of work, and we had already waited too long to begin this final phase, but with luck, no distractions, and gallons of caffeine, we thought we could deliver the report before the deadline, which we had been pointedly told was a firm one.

Which was why I was down in my office on the first floor of our brownstone on West Fifty-sixth Street at five in the morning, calling up notes and numerical data on the computer and working on a first draft. Garth was still asleep up in his apartment on the third floor of the brownstone. My biggest distraction and the love of my life, Dr. Harper Rhys-Whitney, was away searching for new species of poisonous snakes in the Amazon Basin, and Garth's wife, the folksinger Mary Tree, was on a concert tour of Europe to promote her latest album. That left us free to eat junk food, sleep, and work until the job was finished. By then, Harper would be back. We planned to close up the shop for a month or two, and give my secretary, Francisco, a well-deserved paid vacation. Garth would join his wife on tour in Europe, and Harper and I would fly off to some as yet unspecified location that I hoped would be relatively snake-free. After wandering through CIA Ops insanity for well nigh six months, Garth and I needed a long rest, and a little loving to go along with it wasn't going to hurt at all.

At seven I turned on CNN to catch the early morning news, and I found the lead story very disturbing. A Supreme Court justice, Richard Weiner, had been killed in an automobile accident the night before while returning from a bar association dinner at which he had given a speech. Weiner was one of only two justices on the high court who could be described as a stalwart liberal on a court of constantly shifting alignments otherwise comprising three ultra-conservatives and four middle-of-the-roaders whose opinions, at best, were unpredictable on any given issue. From my point of view, Weiner's death was a severe blow to a country where liberal voices, especially those of people in power, were in increasingly dwindling supply. The balance, if it could be called that, of the Supreme Court was now seriously at risk. The sitting president, a moderate who occasionally suffered spasms of liberal thought and action, was fighting like hell to stay in the Oval Office, but not many people thought he could be reelected, and not a few thought his party might even dump him at their convention to be held in New York toward the end of the month. The country was burning with a kind of right-wing fever, and it was hard to find anybody, on the ubiquitous right-wing talk shows or on the stump, who seemed to think that the federal government was good for anything but building more bombers and prisons and providing care and feeding for big business and right-wing politicians. This president, of course, had plenty of time to select a nominee to fill Richard Weiner's seat, but serving up a name—any name— would be a futile gesture. The ultra-conservatives would block any nomination and bide their time until they could get their own man or woman in the presidency, and their own brand of Supreme Court justice, one virtually guaranteed to overturn, or vote to overturn, *Roe v. Wade* at the first opportunity. The president could nominate Thomas Jefferson, and it wouldn't make any difference; the ultra-right wing smelled blood in the water, and they wanted Genghis Khan. The news of Weiner's death was so depressing that I turned off the television.

At 8:45, Francisco, whom I hadn't even heard come in, knocked

at the door, opened it, and stuck his head into my office. The His-
panic, who had worked for me now for almost a decade, was slightly
built and not much taller than I was, and with his new "look"—
slicked-back hair and pencil-thin mustache—he resembled a
pared-down version of Rudolph Valentino. "Excuse me, sir. There's
someone here who'd like to speak to you."

"Who?"

Francisco must have seen the look of annoyance on my face, or
heard it in my voice, because he winced slightly. "He says his name
is Thomas Dickens."

"Francisco, I hope to hell you didn't give anybody an appointment."

"No, sir. He doesn't have an appointment. I think he's on his way
to work."

"What does he want?"

"I don't know, sir. He said Lou Skalin recommended that he talk
to you."

"Tell him I can't do anything for him until the beginning of Octo-
ber, at the earliest. If his business can wait until then, give him an
appointment. Otherwise, give him the names of some of our colleagues."

"Yes, sir," Francisco replied, and started to close the door.

"Hold it," I said curtly, slapping my desk in exasperation and
leaning back in my chair. Lou Skalin was head of the Fortune Society, a New York–based self-help organization of ex-convicts. Garth
and I occasionally did *pro bono* work for them, and, in return, Skalin
had often been an invaluable source of information on any number of
matters. I liked the man, and I didn't want to offend him, even by
proxy. "Send Mr. Dickens in."

"Yes, sir."

I rose from my chair and started around my desk, then almost tripped over my feet in surprise when Thomas Dickens suddenly appeared in the doorway, blocking out the sun. The man was enormous, at least six feet five or six, and upwards of two hundred and fifty pounds, all bulging muscle. His nose appeared to have been broken so many times that it was now a puffy lump of cartilage and bent bone sitting like a ball of dough in the center of his face, which was covered with crude, purplish jailhouse tattoos. He was very big and very black. Except for his eyes, dark pools that glittered with intelligence and seemed sensitive and kind, he had to be the meanest-looking, ugliest man I'd ever seen, and I'd seen more than my share of brutish types. He was wearing the summer uniform of the New York Sanitation Department. Both arms, which bulged out of his short-sleeved shirt, were also covered with old jailhouse tattoos, black on black, wiggling lines of ink carved into his flesh with the point of a shank. He was a truly awesome presence, a kind of moving mountain of graffiti advertising strength and power. In one huge ham of a hand, his left, he carried a black metal lunch pail, and under his right arm was a misshapen, scarred Ralph Lauren leather portfolio that I was pretty certain had been plucked from some pile of trash. He set down the lunch pail, then abruptly walked the rest of the way into my office and extended his hand in a quick, nervous gesture.

"I'm Thomas Dickens, Dr. Frederickson," the man said in a deep, rumbling voice that seemed laced with just a hint of anxiety. "But you can call me Moby. Everybody does. It's a kid's nickname that stuck. I used to be fat as a whale before I went to the joint and got into seriously pumping iron."

I tentatively thrust my hand up into his, and was pleased when he released it with the bones intact. "Moby Dickens. That's, uh . . . right."

"I really appreciate your agreeing to see me," he said quickly, anxiously glancing back over his shoulder as if he was expecting someone to sneak up on him. "It took me a while to work up the courage to come in. I didn't want to call, because I don't speak as well as I write. I'm not good on the phone. I also know I don't make a good first impression—my appearance, I mean. I'm scary-looking, and it puts people off, so I figured I'd just take a chance and drop in on my way to work. Lou told me you're not scared of anything."

"He was talking about my brother."

"Nah. He was talking about you. Anyway, thanks again."

"Well, you haven't scared me yet, Mr. Dickens," I said, toting up my first lie of the day and discounting my first, visceral reaction when I'd seen him filling up my doorway.

"Moby."

"Moby." I pointed to a chair over by my desk that I hoped was strong enough to support him. "Come on over and sit down."

"Thank you, sir," he said, going over to the chair and sitting down, cradling his leather portfolio in both arms. The wood creaked, but the chair held together.

I went back behind my desk and sat down in my swivel chair, resisting the impulse to glance at the data that still flickered, impatiently awaiting my attention, on my computer monitor. "What can I do for you, Moby?"

"Somebody's been stealing my poetry."

"Somebody's been . . . stealing . . . your poetry."

"Here," he said, reaching into his leather portfolio and pulling out a magazine. "I'll show you. Page twenty-three."

He handed over the magazine, which was something called *The New England Journal of Poetry,* and dated two years before. I opened it to page twenty-three and saw a poem there entitled "Fountainhead," by Thomas Dickens:

I had escaped that hell riding
The backs of my demons,
Smoothing the way with paving
Stone words plucked from
The storm, cemented together
With my tears that otherwise
Would have dropped to waste,
Soaking the ground,
Miring my tongue.

Fear whispers from a far place
Deeper still than the
Cacophonous, rain-swept
Arena of our hatred,
A quiet hole where there
Is no wind and even our
Screams are drowned
In the silent sea.

"Very nice," I said, glancing up into the scarred, mashed, and tattooed face of the man sitting across from me.

"Thank you."

I looked to my right as Garth, dressed in shorts and a T-shirt and carrying the fistful of papers he had taken up to his apartment the night before, entered the office. He stopped when he saw us. "Sorry," he said, taking a pencil from between his teeth. "I didn't know you had anybody in here with you."

"What's up?"

"I need to call up the names of all those shell corporations, and Francisco's using his terminal to do something else for me. It'll wait. I'll come back when you're finished."

"It's all right," I said, getting up and coming around from behind the desk. "This won't take much longer, and we can move over to the couch. Garth Frederickson, this is Moby Dickens. Somebody has been stealing Mr. Dickens' poetry."

I thought Garth might be as amused as I was by the name, or show some sign of interest in the situation, but my brother was either being polite or was totally distracted by his paper pursuit of the CIA's dummy companies, because he displayed no reaction at all. He sat down behind my desk, brushed a few stray strands of his shoulder-length, wheat-colored hair away from his eyes, then began a brutal attack on my keyboard using the index finger of each hand.

I motioned Moby Dickens over to the small couch set up along the wall of the office, to the left of my desk, and he went over and sat down on it. He filled most of the couch, so I pulled up the single chair and sat down in front of him. He once again reached into the cracked leather folds of his portfolio and pulled out another magazine. This one was called *The Raging River Review,* and was printed on much cheaper paper than the first journal he had shown me, with the pages stapled together. It was dated six months before. He opened the magazine to a page, handed it to me. There was a poem entitled "Fright," by Jefferson Kelly:

> Speaks softly
> From a distant place
> Even deeper than the
> Cacophonous, rain-swept
> Arena of our hatred;
> A still hole where there
> Is no breeze and even our
> Screams are drowned
> Out by the
> Din of silence.

"It's yours," I said, handing him back the magazine.

Moby Dickens nodded, then plucked out a half dozen other magazines and offered them to me. "There are a lot more—"

"I get the idea," I said, holding up my hand. "This Jefferson Kelly reads a poem of yours in some literary journal, then alters it slightly and submits it as his own work to some other magazine. It's plagiarism."

"Yes."

"And you want some kind of compensation."

The ex-convict with the tattooed face and doughboy nose replaced the magazines in his portfolio, then studied me with his bright, expressive dark eyes. He seemed surprised. "No, sir," he said at last. "It's not about money. I just want him to stop."

"Aha."

"A number of editors have been publishing my work for a few years, and so they're familiar with my name and work. It was one of them who noticed a plagiarized poem in one of the other journals, and she first brought it to my attention by sending me a copy. Then I went through the literature and found that this Kelly has plagiarized at least a dozen of my poems. There could be more—there are hundreds of literary and so-called 'little' magazines, some of which are just run off on mimeograph machines in somebody's basement, and it's impossible to check all of them. I can prove all the poems are mine, because mine were always published first. He may copy other people's poems as well, and then submit them as his own work. I don't know. I just want him to stop copying mine. My editors should be cooperative. I was hoping you could find out who this Jefferson Kelly is and where he lives, and you could go talk to him."

"Why wouldn't these editors who know your work and realize it's been plagiarized cooperate with you? One of them might be able to give you a return address for this Kelly, maybe even a phone number.

You could talk to him yourself." I paused, smiled. "Moby, trust me on this: Kelly finding you on his doorstep would be much more of an incentive for him to do the right thing than finding me. The sight of you will positively fire his imagination. I guarantee he'll stop copying your poems."

I thought it a perfectly sensible suggestion, and I even thought Moby Dickens might be amused by my dry wit. But he didn't smile. Shadows moved in his eyes, and he looked away. "I don't want to do that," he said softly.

"Uh, why not? He's been ripping off your work to pass himself off as a poet. You have every right to confront him. That's what you want me to do, and I'm telling you that you'd be a far more effective spokesman for your cause. One mild glower should do the trick. Even half a glance."

"I don't like to glower. I don't want to use my body to defend my poetry."

"What's the difference between using your body and hiring mine, aside from the fact that you'll save money? I hope it won't come as a shock to you to be told that your body is a lot more persuasive-looking than mine."

Not only did I fail to get an affirmation of my sound logic and prudent fiscal advice, I still couldn't get even a smile out of the man. "You don't understand," he said in the same soft tone, lowering his head. When he raised it again, I was thoroughly startled to see that his eyes were misted with tears.

"Moby," I said quickly, "I wasn't making fun of your physical appearance. I was just stating a fact. And I didn't mean to be insensitive. If that's how it sounded, I apologize."

He took a deep breath, shook his head, and said, "I killed a man in a bar fight down in Mississippi when I was seventeen years old. It was self-defense, but I got fifteen to twenty anyway. But the truth is that being sent to prison saved my life; the way I was heading, I'd have been dead by the time I was twenty. Being put in prison was a gift, because it was there that I found my gift. My muse came to me in prison. I discovered that I could take everyday words, change them around and polish them and make them into something beautiful. I discovered I had a beautiful soul, and it was made out of poems. Dr. Frederickson, before prison I thought I had to be a badass motherfucker because I *looked* like a badass motherfucker—fat, ugly, and mean. But that wasn't true. Through my poems, I could look at my soul and see it all naked, pure, and . . . true. My poetry is all I ever want my editors and readers to see. I've never spoken to an editor on the phone, and I've turned down dozens of invitations to lunch, and even to visit colleges and speak to students. I know what I look like. I don't want anyone to see that, or to know that Thomas Dickens is an ex-convict garbageman in New York City. I'm not ashamed of who I am, or my job—I make a decent living. But it would be a *distraction* from what I've created if anyone were to find out more about me. Maybe that will change in time, but that's how I feel now. I'm afraid I couldn't write anymore if people found out about me. I especially don't want this thief, Jefferson Kelly, to know anything about me personally. That's why I need somebody to do this thing for me."

"Moby," I said, suppressing a sigh, "how much money are we talking about here? I mean, how much have you earned from your poetry?"

He stared at me for some time in silence, as if confused by the question. "I don't know," he said at last. "A few dollars, probably less than a hundred. Most of the magazines pay in copies or subscriptions."

"Let me be blunt with you, Moby. All of the money you've earned from your poetry over the years probably wouldn't pay for an hour of my time. I don't think—"

"I can pay!" he snapped, his voice suddenly booming in the small office. Now his eyes glinted with anger. "I told you this wasn't about money!"

I cleared my throat, stood up. "I didn't mean to offend you, Moby. I can see that you're upset about this, and under other circumstances I wouldn't hesitate to take on the assignment. But the fact of the matter is that Garth and I are up to our eyeballs in work right now, and I just don't have the time to take on anything else. We haven't accepted new cases for months now. My secretary will give you the names of some other—"

"Excuse me!" Garth said sharply.

I turned around in my chair, and was somewhat surprised to find my brother standing up behind my desk. His hands were on his hips, and he was glaring at me. "Garth?"

"I want to talk to you, Brother."

"Sure, Garth," I replied, puzzled by my brother's interruption and demeanor. "Just give me a couple of minutes to get Mr. Dickens squared away."

"Right now," Garth said curtly, walking briskly to the door and motioning with his hand for me to follow him. He looked at Moby Dickens, and his manner changed abruptly. He smiled easily, and his tone was positively sweet as he continued, "Just stay where you are, Mr. Dickens. The good doctor will be back in his office in a couple of minutes."

Even more puzzled, I followed Garth out of my office and into the larger office in front of it that served as our reception area. Garth nodded to Francisco, who quickly rose from where he sat before his computer terminal and walked out into the hallway, closing the door behind him.

"I should kick your ass," Garth said as he turned to me. His voice had become soft and even, the tone he used when he was seriously upset about something. "In fact, I think I'm going to. Definitely. I don't see how I can stop myself."

"Huh?"

"What have we got to do that's more important than putting a stop to the theft of a man's soul?"

"Uh . . . helping to bury the CIA? You know how I hate these trick questions."

"You've been spending too much time taking fifteen hundred dollars a day of the taxpayers' money, Brother. It's made you arrogant and insensitive. You'd better run your own soul check. I remember a time not so long ago, when I was still a cop and you were a college professor your colleagues laughed at for trying to moonlight as a private investigator, when you'd have slobbered with gratitude over anybody who walked through that door to offer you some business."

"Garth, this is no time to get squirrelly on me. We're involved in the most important investigation of our lives, and we've got less than three weeks to wrap it all up and submit a comprehensive report."

"The CIA business is important, but it's not important. It's only important because we've chosen to make it seem so."

"Well, thank you, Carlos Castaneda."

"Not Carlos Castaneda—Mongo Frederickson. And you got the notion from our mother. Who was it who always used to say that, finally, the only thing an individual can do to make the world a better place is to lead a life of honesty and good deeds? Remember Mom telling us how failing to do the right thing at the moment it must be done puts a little crack in the world where good leaks out and evil seeps in? There was a time when you understood that. It's not some outfit called the CIA that's a problem, but certain *people in* the CIA. How many of those people do you really think we're going to nail? Even if the CIA were completely demolished, most of the bad folks over there are just going to end up doing bad things someplace else. Take the last election."

"You take the last election."

Garth ignored the remark and stepped closer. "If a significant number of Americans keep kicking over rocks and electing to office whatever crawls out from under, what do you think you're going to do about it? The people we have now in Washington have managed to poison the atmosphere in this country, and the change could be permanent—CIA or no CIA. It wasn't the CIA that elected those creeps."

"It was CIA money that helped elect a lot of them."

"It was ordinary Americans who pulled the levers in their voting booths. But who knows? Maybe the changes aren't permanent. Before those fools totally dismantle the government, people may get tired of their right-wing bullshit and elect people to office who'll give us the kind of left-wing bullshit you and I love to hear. The point is that there's nothing you can really do about it, which means it's *not important*. Thomas Dickens' problem, however, *is* important, because it matters, and because there *is* something you can do about it. There's a great white whale, of sorts, sitting back there in your office, and you'd best not let it swim away with its wounds unattended."

"Jesus, you're really pulling out all the oratorical stops. That's outrageous."

"It's true."

"Dickens' problem really is important to you, isn't it?"

"You noticed. It should also be important to you."

"Garth, do you really think our role in the CIA investigation is so *unimportant* that we should risk missing a tight deadline to go off chasing after some poem-robber?"

"Hey, the company has fucked me over every bit as much as it has you—maybe more. And, in the final analysis, I still say Dickens' problem is more important. But it doesn't have to be that complicated. What's the big deal? Call a couple of his editors and see if one of them has a submission envelope with this Jefferson Kelly's return address on it, and we proceed from there. Francisco can do it."

I thought about it for a few seconds, shrugged. "Hey, when you're right, you're right."

"Damn right I'm right. You wouldn't have needed me to explain it to you if you hadn't become such a self-important little prick whose ass I'm probably still going to have to kick."

"Garth, I really hope this doesn't mean you're losing enthusiasm for our other little task at hand."

Garth smiled thinly. "Not in the least. Now that we've addressed Moby Dickens' concerns, serious thumping on the CIA suddenly seems very important to me again. It's what Mr. Castaneda would call 'controlled folly.' Among other things, I still owe them for costing me a career I wasn't ready to give up at the time, and almost getting the both of us killed on more than a few occasions. Now go do some good before I thump on you."

"Yes, *sir.* Thank you, *sir.*"

I went back into my office and found Moby Dickens sitting on the edge of the couch staring at the floor, nervously rubbing his enormous hands together. I walked over to him and put a hand on his shoulder. "We're going to see what we can do for you, Moby."

"Thank you," he rumbled, then got to his feet and reached for his wallet.

"You don't have to give us any money now, Moby. We'll bill you for our hours after we get the job done. Here's what you can do for us. Give me copies of all the poems you've written that you know Kelly has plagiarized, along with the magazines that have his versions in them. I need the dates each poem appeared."

"I've already done that, Dr. Frederickson," he said quickly, picking up his portfolio from the couch and holding it open for me to see. "It's all in here. I've catalogued and cross-referenced everything."

"Good. Then I want the names and addresses—and telephone numbers, if you have them—of every editor who's ever published your work, and the same for the editors who've published Kelly's smudge jobs. I'm particularly interested in the editors you've communicated with and who might help us track down Kelly. The editor who first put you on to Kelly should be at the top of the list."

"I've done that too, sir," he said, hefting the leather pouch in his hands. "It's all in here, along with a copy of *Poet's Market.* That lists the names of editors and addresses of all the magazines that publish poetry. I've highlighted the editors I've dealt with, and cross-indexed them with my poems and Kelly's plagiarisms."

"Outstanding."

"If you can just find this man, talk to him and make him see how important my work is to me. I'm afraid that, someday, people who've read both my work and his versions will look at me and believe I plagiarized his poems, not the other way around. All I want is for him to stop doing it, sir."

"You've got it. And accomplished poets like yourself get to call me Mongo—in fact, it's required."

For the first time since he'd entered my office, Moby Dickens smiled. He must have received reasonably good dental care in prison, because his teeth were white and even, with a gap between the two front ones. "Okay, Mongo. This means a great deal to me."

"Drop your portfolio off with Francisco at the front desk on your way out, along with your address and a telephone number where we can reach you. I'll be in touch."

He shook my hand again, then, still grinning, turned and walked out. I went back to my computer to call back up the notes and data I had been working on, then went out into the hallway to look for Garth. He must have gone back up to his apartment to work, because there was no sign of him. I went into the front office, and Francisco looked up from his computer terminal. Moby Dickens' worn leather portfolio was on the desk beside him.

"Francisco," I said, walking over to him and putting a hand on one of his frail shoulders, "give Margaret a call and see what she's up to. If she's not working, see if she can come in and handle the office for a few days. Otherwise, call in a temp. Make sure he or she is good, because he'll be doing your job."

My secretary frowned slightly. "You're firing me, sir?"

"Hardly. I'm temporarily promoting you to the rank of Associate Investigator."

Now he grinned. "Really? What do you want me to do, sir?"

"Find me a plagiarist."

# CHAPTER 4

*I* *had green tea and cold sesame noodles for lunch at my desk,* working my way through the reams of notes and data. Most of the "records" we had obtained from the Aristide government—everything from military and police payrolls to the sundry contents of government filing cabinets—were written in longhand, and it had taken the combined, full-time efforts of three translators just to decipher what we had. Next had come the not inconsiderable task of transcribing it all into computerese so that the information could be sorted and analyzed and finally called forth to form charts and graphs which we hoped, in the end, would paint a very damning portrait of an entire, brutalized country essentially owned and operated by the CIA, the poorest of nations serving as a mysterious conduit for billions of dollars which could not be accounted for in any CIA budget. This phase wasn't the most stimulating work, but it had to be done, for if the CIA was to be brought down, it had to be accomplished with numbers and the irrefutable testimony of witnesses, not the Frederickson brothers jumping up and down and screaming hysterically about the bloody deeds of a bunch of savage killers, many of whom seemed to be monumentally stupid, whose salaries were paid by the American people. The blade of the saber with which we hoped to decapitate the company had to be ice cold.

Garth entered the office in late afternoon. He was carrying a large manila envelope which he was in the process of opening. "Just arrived by messenger," he said, tearing open the envelope. "Figured we'd check it out together."

I watched as he spread the edges of the envelope and peered inside. "Well?"

His answer was to take out the contents and hand them to me. They were two enlarged copies of photographs. One was a duplicate of the head-and-shoulders shot of the triangular-faced man with the piercing eyes that had been displayed on the altar in the basement of General Vilair Michel's house, and the other was a wide-angle shot of the altar itself, as it had appeared when we'd first discovered it. A note clipped to one of the photos read:

> Good hunting. Hope you nail the bastards.
>
> Carl Beauvil

"*Voilà,*" I said, glancing back up at Garth.

"Yeah," Garth replied with a shrug. "Nice of Beauvil to come through for us like this, but we probably should have told him that our curiosity was a lot bigger than our capacity to try to do anything with this stuff. We've got no time to try to track down this guy. We've got all we can do to organize and tie together the information we've already got."

"You're right," I said, reluctantly tossing the photographs onto my desk.

"Let's go get something to eat."

"I figured I'd have Francisco call out for a pizza before he goes home."

Garth shook his head, then grabbed the front of my shirt and pulled me up out of my chair. "Come on. I'll buy you a steak. We both need a break. There's nothing our company friends would like better than for one or the both of us to keel over from exhaustion and malnutrition before we can finish this thing."

"In that case, I'll take you up on your offer of a steak. But only for medicinal purposes."

Over drinks and dinner we discussed literary strategy, the actual form of our report, and the order of its contents. I wanted to start off with what I considered the good stuff, offering up front a lurid account of the voodoo-style ritual murders that had thwarted our interrogation of six key witnesses to CIA-sponsored atrocities in Haiti and elsewhere. Garth was against that approach, pointing out that we could prove no link whatsoever between the voodoo hit squad and the CIA, and arguing that such an approach would only give the CIA's allies an opportunity to start shouting "preposterous" and "sensationalism" at the outset, charging that we were not serious people if we were willing to make such unsubstantiated charges, and therefore nothing we had to say could be trusted. Calling the meeting to order with entrails, he argued, would only serve to undermine the scant and precious hard proof we did have.

My resistance was feeble, because I knew all along he was right. We agreed we would start with a brief and dry introduction, vaguely outlining what we hoped to show, then immediately offer up our hard data, progressively working our way through the anecdotal portions of our investigation results where the leads were tantalizing but the evidence as yet unsubstantiated, awaiting the attention of congressional committees with subpoena powers, and then give them a boffo ending, serving up the blood and gore in an appendix, nicely bracketed by financial charts and tables listing all the suspected dummy corporations that were bastard children of the CIA.

When we arrived back at the brownstone I was startled to see a very well-known figure sitting on our stoop, casually smoking a cigarette. Lucas Tremayne was the Academy Award–winning writer and director of one of the highest-grossing films of the past decade, and a very high-profile social activist. The lean, handsome man with the graying crew cut was anything but a Hollywood type. He was rarely seen in public, and when he was it was usually because he was lending his celebrity to promote one of his favorite causes, such as increased funding for AIDS research, or some charity event. In the news clips and photos I had seen of him, he was usually dressed as he was now, in faded jeans, soft leather boots, denim shirt, and Mets baseball cap.

Garth appeared slightly unsettled but not surprised at the film director's presence. "Hello, Lucas," my brother said as the man ground out his cigarette and stood up.

"Good to see you, Garth," Tremayne said, stepping down onto the sidewalk and shaking my brother's hand. "Now I know where you've been hiding out for the past few months."

"Lucas Tremayne, this is my brother, Mongo."

"A pleasure," the director said, extending his hand and removing his cap. In the glow from the streetlight I could see that his gray eyes almost perfectly matched his hair, and his smile was easy and friendly. "I've heard a great deal about you."

"Likewise, and likewise."

Garth said, "Lucas is a friend and neighbor."

Lucas Tremayne released my hand, then turned to my brother. When he spoke again, there was a slightly accusatory tone to his voice. "I haven't seen you around Cairn in a while."

Garth shrugged. "Yeah, well, Mary's been off on an extended tour promoting her new album, so I've been staying here at the brownstone to save myself the commute."

"I've been keeping an eye on your house."

"I appreciate that, Lucas."

"I also notice that the Cairn police have been patrolling past there pretty often. I guess they know the house is empty most of the time."

Garth merely shrugged again. He seemed increasingly uncomfortable, as if he knew Tremayne was leading up to something he didn't want to talk about.

"Garth, can I have a few words with you?"

"Of course," my brother said, motioning for Tremayne to precede us up the steps. "Come on up to my apartment and we'll have a drink."

I walked up the stairs after the two men, and when we reached the door to Garth's apartment on the third-floor landing I paused and held out my hand to the film director. "I'll say good night, folks. Lucas, keep up the good work."

"Mongo, I'd like to talk to you too."

"Sure," I said, and followed him in as Garth held the door open.

We went into the living room. Tremayne and I sat at opposite ends of the sofa while Garth made drinks at the bar and brought them to us. Tremayne set his aside untouched. "I was talking to Carl Beauvil this afternoon, Garth," he said quietly. The vaguely accusatory tone had returned to his voice. "We were together at a fund-raising event for Haitian refugees. He told me what happened in Spring Valley, and he told me what the two of you are up to."

Garth grunted. "That detective certainly is a talkative chap. The last thing he mentioned to us was that we shouldn't even admit to ever being in Spring Valley, much less discuss what happened while we were there."

"Carl is Haitian, you know," Tremayne said, turning to me and fixing me with his gray eyes. His expression was now somber.

"I'd assumed as much."

"He and I go back a ways, ever since I moved to Cairn with my family a few years ago. We've worked together closely on a number of projects. He trusts me, which is why he told me what he did. He knows what he said would be held in confidence. He didn't know your brother and I are friends. What you told him disturbed him a great deal."

Garth turned in his chair to look at me. "Lucas is extremely active in the Haitian community on behalf of refugees, Mongo. He lends his name and prestige to their cause. He's also a noted collector of Haitian art."

"I see," I said in a neutral tone. I was beginning to understand why the film director's sudden appearance on our stoop had made my brother uncomfortable.

Tremayne cleared his throat, leaned forward with his elbows on his knees, and clasped his hands together. "Garth, Carl tells me you and Mongo have been working on this Haiti investigation for months. I can't believe you didn't mention it to me."

"There are a number of very good reasons, Lucas," my brother replied evenly.

"You know how I feel about Haiti and Haitians, and the oppression they've suffered for so long. You also know how hard I've worked on their behalf. *I've* always suspected the CIA was involved in things over there right up to their slimy eyeballs, all the way back to Papa Doc and his Ton-ton Macoutes. Christ, I never dreamed anybody would ever actually try to prove it and do something about it. I want to help."

"There's nothing for you to do, Lucas."

"No? I'll bet I know a hell of a lot more Haitians than you do."

"That's one of the reasons I didn't say anything to you. Mongo and I don't want what we're doing to be widely advertised."

"I can be discreet."

"It's dangerous business, Lucas."

"Do I come off as a coward to you?"

"Hardly. But that's not the point. No matter how discreet you may be, asking questions about the CIA and the former rulers of Haiti would be sure to attract the attention of the wrong people. You have more than yourself to worry about. Your wife and children live in Cairn, and you have a very busy career to attend to. These people we're after take no prisoners. The man who was murdered in Spring Valley was a potential informer. The CIA knew that, and their people got to him one step ahead of us. He was killed not only to silence him, but also to send out a message to other Haitians who might be willing to give us information. There's a kind of voodoo hit squad out there, and the Spring Valley man was their sixth victim. Part of the idea is to spread terror in the Haitian community. If you get into the act, these people would be delighted to kill you. Murdering a famous Hollywood director well known for his commitment to Haitian causes would be a perfect way to permanently scare off remaining potential witnesses who otherwise might be persuaded to testify before any congressional committees that may decide to hold hearings as a result of our report. If Detective Beauvil provided you with any details about this murder, then you know these people do bad things to the bodies of their victims, before and after death. It would haunt your wife and kids for the rest of their lives. I didn't say anything to you because I knew what your reaction would be, and there was—is—no reason to put you in harm's way."

Lucas Tremayne had gone slightly pale, but his voice was steady when he said, "You and Mongo don't look any the worse for wear, and you've been working on this for half a year."

"Mongo and I do this sort of thing for a living. We're armed to the teeth, and we're constantly surveying our surroundings and thinking about our safety, not scripts and camera angles. Also, we enjoy a kind of limited professional immunity. Kill you, and the publicity focus would be on your links to Haiti and how the generals or ex–Ton-ton

Macoutes or Fraph finally gave you some payback. It would scare Haitians. Kill us, and the focus would be on what we were doing that got us killed—namely investigating the CIA's links to Haiti. We keep backup copies of all our files and records in a safe deposit box that we feed every night. Our murders would seriously piss off a lot of important people, and get lots of publicity that would result in a lot of investigative reporting. That scares the CIA; they want to head us off at the pass, not have the mountain fall on them. Publicity about *them* is precisely what they're trying to avoid. Besides, Lucas, the issue is moot. We're finished with our field work. Now it's just a matter of tying together what we've got and writing up our report."

"I hear what you're saying," Tremayne said quietly. "But there still must be some way I can be useful. You need somebody to answer your phone? Type up the report?"

Garth glanced at me and raised his eyebrows slightly, then set his drink down and got up from his chair. "Excuse me for a couple of minutes."

My brother left the room, and Lucas Tremayne and I stared at each other. Finally I said, "Making that last film of yours was a gutsy thing to do. Its subject isn't exactly a favorite topic of conversation. If it hadn't been the success it was, it could have seriously damaged your career."

The film director shrugged, smiled thinly. "I do what I can for people and causes I care about—just like you and Garth do. All I did was make a movie on a controversial subject nobody wants to talk about. I think what *you're* doing is incredibly gutsy, and I'm not sure I buy what Garth told me about your professional immunity. You've surely been in danger from the first day you started working on this project."

"Oh, I'm sure the company would be delighted if we fell off a cliff or got run over by a truck—just as long as it didn't point to them. But we're being well paid for the risk."

"I don't believe you're doing it for money."

He had that right. Diddling the CIA, or trying to, was a labor of love—but for reasons that had to remain secret. "Garth meant no disrespect by not mentioning this Haiti investigation to you."

"I understand, Mongo."

"I mean no disrespect either, but Beauvil really had no business discussing this with a civilian. Whatever his feelings or reasons, he could have put you at risk. Do you understand why you should keep all this to yourself? You shouldn't even discuss this with your family—especially not with your family."

Tremayne colored slightly, but he didn't protest. Finally he nodded at me and flashed a grin. "I've been following your exploits for some time—even before Garth and I became friends. You're quite a celebrity yourself."

"Yeah. You think the world is ready for a big-budget film about a dwarf private detective? I see Schwarzenegger in the lead, with maybe DeVito playing Garth."

He laughed. "I think it's a wonderful idea. I'm going to pitch it to Arnold and Danny the next time I see them."

Garth walked back into the room. He was carrying the photographs Carl Beauvil had sent us. He selected the head-and-shoulders shot of the man in the priest's collar, handed it to Tremayne. "Like you said, you know a hell of a lot of Haitians. Ever see this guy before?"

The man with the gray eyes and hair barely glanced at the photograph before looking back up at Garth. "I've not only seen him, but I know him personally."

Well, well, well. I drained off the rest of the Scotch in my glass, rose to get some more.

"Who is he?" Garth asked.

"Guy Fournier—Dr. Guy Fournier. He's Haitian, a defrocked Roman Catholic priest who was an antigovernment activist in Haiti long before Aristide arrived on the scene, and long before me. His life must certainly have been at risk, for years, and it was probably only his collar that saved him; the past Haitian governments and the Roman Catholic hierarchy in Haiti have always had what you might call a close working relationship."

"Not only the governments," Garth said dryly. "Not a few of those friendly neighborhood padres have turned up on lists of paid CIA informers."

"It doesn't surprise me. Fournier also happens to be a collector of Haitian art, which is how I know him. We go to a lot of the same galleries, shows, and auctions."

I took a long pull at my second drink, sat back down on the couch. "Why was he defrocked?"

"Ostensibly for preaching liberation theology, which was the same as heresy to the hierarchy. But the real reason they defrocked him was to remove a thorn in their side and make him a softer target for Fraph thugs. They considered him a real pain in the ass. Friends helped him get out of the country a few months before Aristide was restored to power. Otherwise, he would have ended up getting his arms and legs cut off in Fort Dimanche. He lives right here in New York. His Ph.D. is in comparative religion, and that's what he teaches now, downtown at Mongo's former place of employment."

Garth asked, "Why didn't Beauvil recognize him?"

"I can't be certain, but probably because Carl has never lived in Haiti. He was born here. Fournier wasn't that well known outside of Haiti. Also, Carl's a policeman, and that's not a profession most Haitians have a lot of use for. They're afraid of the police. Carl does an enormous amount of work for his people, but he's still essentially isolated within the community. He's probably never even heard of Fournier. Incidentally, this looks like it could be a surveillance photo taken by the army, Fraph, or the police over there. May I ask where you got it?"

I said, "It was on a voodoo altar in the basement of the murder victim's home in Spring Valley."

Lucas Tremayne frowned slightly. "That's odd."

"Why?"

"I don't know. I'm no expert on voodoo, but a voodoo altar just seems an odd place to find a picture of a Roman Catholic priest. Could it have been set down there by chance, by accident?"

"No," Garth replied, and handed his friend the second photograph. "This is a picture of the altar itself. You can see that this man's photograph is placed right in the middle, in the center of that circle of candles, carvings, and painted symbols, with the cross beneath it. Mean anything to you?"

Tremayne shook his head in disgust, then pursed his lips slightly. "I hate this voodoo shit. It's probably done more harm to the Haitian people than the generals, Fraph, and Ton-ton Macoutes, who've all used voodoo as a weapon against the people. It's a self-inflicted wound. I do recognize some of these things around the photograph as voodoo fetishes. They mean something."

I grunted. "The question is, what?"

"May I keep this photograph of the altar?"

"No," Garth said, reaching out to retrieve both photographs from the other man's hand.

"I may not be an expert on voodoo, but I'm certain I can find somebody who is."

"You flash that photograph around, and you're likely to conjure up some people you really don't want to meet. Among other bad habits they have, they cut out people's hearts."

"Garth, I'm not going to flash—"

"Say good night, Lucas," Garth said with a thin smile, gently but firmly grasping his friend's elbow and lifting him up off the sofa. "Mongo and I have to get our beauty rest."

"But I want to find out more about this for you!"

"Nope. Not a word to anyone. You've already been more than helpful in identifying this Guy Fournier for us. Mongo and I don't have time to track down any more leads even if you could produce them for us, and I'm sure the Spring Valley police and FBI are following up. Safe trip home."

"But I haven't finished my drink!"

"Not to worry; Mongo will finish it for you."

We walked with Tremayne to the parking garage in the next block where he had left his car. After he paid the attendant, he turned to shake hands, and said, "Look, I'm sorry for barging in on you guys like that. I tried calling you right after I left the reception where I talked to Carl, but your secretary had gone home, and I didn't know what message to leave. Then I got antsy, so I just drove in on the chance I'd catch up with you."

"Jesus, Lucas," Garth said, squeezing the other man's shoulder, "don't apologize. We might never have identified this Fournier. He could provide us with a few telling details we don't have now, and he might prove to be a valuable witness later on."

"You think so?"

"We'll see—you won't. Good night, my friend."

Lucas Tremayne waved to us as he got into his Range Rover when it was brought to him, then drove off. I turned to Garth. "Time pressure or no, we've got to go for it, right?"

"Sure. Like I told Lucas, Fournier might be able to connect some of the dots we're writing up right now."

"You go talk to him. I'm about ten times faster on the computer than you are."

"No, you go. Academe is your province, and he'll have heard your name bandied about more than once in those hallowed halls. He'll be more comfortable with you. Besides, I'm on the verge of a breakthrough; I think I'm about ready to begin using four fingers."

# CHAPTER 5

*D*r. *Guy Fournier's office at the university was on the third* floor of a four-story, rather nondescript building called Faul Hall on the southwest edge of the sprawling campus in lower Manhattan, just off Washington Square. I had decidedly mixed feelings upon returning to the university where I had worked for so many years at a job I'd loved, abruptly walking away because of an act of betrayal, one of a series of betrayals that had almost cost Garth and me our lives. I was early for our appointment, and the door was open, so I went in. The office was rather long and narrow, with two walls taken up by floor-to-ceiling built-in bookcases crammed full of books in English and French. There was a small wooden desk to the left of the doorway, and its surface was piled high with a clutter of student papers and books festooned with multicolored book markers. A gleaming computer workstation was set up against the opposite wall, next to a dirt-streaked window that looked out on a fire escape and a view of the campus that would have been more pleasant if the window hadn't been so dirty. The workstation and its cleared perimeter comprised the only neat area in the office; the floor was littered with stalagmite-like stacks of more books and old magazines, also in English and French. It looked more like a neglected storage area than a place to meet students. I sat down on a stack of ancient *National Geographic*s and waited.

Dr. Guy Fournier arrived precisely at 11:15, the appointed time. His office might be shabby, but he was not. The white-haired man wore sharply creased black slacks, expensive black loafers, and a lightweight gray blazer over a white cotton turtleneck. The man had presence. He was a little over six feet, and stood very erect, almost as if he were at attention. In person, his large, gleaming black eyes in the triangular face were even more striking than in his photograph, which had apparently been taken a few years before. I put him in his early sixties.

"A pleasure to meet you, Dr. Fournier," I said, rising off the magazines and extending my hand. "I'm Robert Frederickson. I very much appreciate your agreeing to see me. Your door was open, so I came in. I hope you don't mind."

"The pleasure is mine, Dr. Frederickson," he said in a rich baritone that was pleasantly laced with a rather lilting Creole accent. He set down a worn leather briefcase on top of a stack of papers on his desk, moved across the room, and turned around the chair at the computer workstation so that it was facing the desk. "My door is always open, especially to such a distinguished visitor as yourself. Please sit down."

I did, pulling the chair even closer. Fournier went behind his desk and settled himself into a wooden swivel chair that creaked as he leaned back and crossed his legs, folding his hands with their long fingers across his flat stomach. "Dr. Robert Frederickson," he continued, smiling easily. "Mongo le Magnifique—the name you used when you were a star with the Statler Brothers Circus. Your friends still call you Mongo. Criminologist, ex–college professor who taught at this very university, black-belt karate expert, private investigator *extraordinaire*. Along with your brother, an ex–police detective, you have been involved in some most unusual—one might even say bizarre—cases. I particularly enjoyed reading about your exploits with that previously unknown creature."

"You seem to know a lot about me."

He shrugged. "Doesn't everyone? As you can see by looking around you, I read a lot, and you are a celebrity. *Time* magazine once referred to you as 'the deadly dwarf.'"

"I must have missed that issue."

"People here still talk about you all the time. It seems you were an extremely popular professor, always playing to a packed house. And you knew your stuff, used to publish a lot of research papers. There are wild rumors, but nobody seems to know for certain the reason you left. You and your brother are currently working as part of a Presidential Commission examining the CIA. Your particular assignment is to investigate and attempt to document alleged illegal activities by the CIA in Haiti."

"I'm impressed. May I ask how you know all this, Doctor?"

"The formation of the Presidential Commission was never formally announced, but its existence and task are no secret to people who follow politics closely. It was reported in both *The New York Times* and *The Washington Post*. Also, I'm quite active in Haitian affairs in this country. What you're doing is common knowledge in the Haitian community throughout this country. We—most of us, that is—appreciate what you and the president are trying to do. There is much hope for righting great wrongs, but there is also a good deal of terror. Hope is not a feeling that comes easily to my people; it has been crushed, along with their bodies, too many times. News of what has happened to people who spoke to you—or who might have been willing to speak to you—has traveled fast. I'm afraid you'll meet with considerable resistance from any remaining witnesses you wish to talk to."

"Actually, we're in the process of wrapping things up."

"Yet you are here, and I assume your visit is in connection with your investigation. As for myself, I am not afraid. I would love nothing better than to help bring the CIA criminals to justice; they helped

ruin my country. Unfortunately, despite my extensive experience
with the dupes of these criminals, any hard evidence of criminal activity I have is probably considerably less than any hard evidence
you now have. I can regale you for hours with some blood-chilling
stories, but my guess is that you've already heard all of them. If
you've come to me for some kind of documentation, I'm afraid you've
wasted your time. As I'm sure you're aware, I was considered a
pariah, and officials of the Church, government, and army did not exactly whisper secrets in my ear. However, I will try to answer any
questions you may have, and I will be more than happy to appear as
a witness at congressional hearings to testify to atrocities I have
seen—but I can't prove any connection to the CIA."

"That's very decent and courageous of you, Professor. I'll dis-
creetly pass along your offer to the head of the commission, who'll
keep it in the strictest confidence. Actually, I've come to see you
about another matter."

The man with the coal-black eyes and mesmerizing gaze frowned
slightly. "Oh? And what would that be?"

"I wanted to ask if you have any idea why someone would place
your photograph on a voodoo altar."

Fournier leaned forward in his chair, resting his elbows on the
desk and lacing his long fingers together under his narrow chin. "My
photograph on a voodoo altar?"

"Yes, sir. In the place of honor, if you will—right in the center. You
seemed to be the point of the display."

He lowered his gaze, sighed, shook his head slightly. "This is very
embarrassing."

"Why is that, sir?"

Fournier looked back up, smiled wryly. "Haiti is a Catholic country, as I'm sure you know, Dr. Frederickson. Virtually everyone is
Catholic. But Haiti is also, as you know, the home of a panoply of pa-

gan practices transplanted there by African slaves, a belief system Americans call voodoo. Unfortunately, many ordinary Haitians tend to mix the two belief systems—voodoo and Catholicism; Catholic saints become voodoo saints, and vice versa. Haitians see no contradiction. Voodoo is very old, and it's embedded in the fabric of our society. I was known as a political dissident and a fighter for the rights of the underclass—which is ninety-nine percent of our people. I was considered by many people to be a hero, and now, apparently, one of those misguided souls has promoted me to saint. The person was probably using my photograph as an object of worship."

"That doesn't seem likely in this case."

"Oh?"

"The guy who had your picture on his altar was an ex-general by the name of Vilair Michel, a murderer and torturer who ran Fort Dimanche for a while. He was in this country illegally. You wouldn't exactly have been a hero to him, much less a saint. His background indicates he'd have preferred to have your head on a platter rather than as an object of worship on an altar. I'd have liked to ask him myself what it was all about, but when we found him his heart had been cut out."

"Another one," Fournier said, grimacing and turning his head away sharply. "That's disgusting."

"He was a mess, all right."

"I hadn't heard about this one. When did the murder take place?"

"It's a fresh kill."

Fournier shook his head, looked back at me. "Another potential witness?"

"Yes. Finding your photograph on a voodoo altar in Michel's house is just a loose end—a curiosity, really. It's a long shot that it means anything that could be useful to us, but I thought it was worth taking a subway ride to check it out."

He again shrugged his shoulders. "I'm sorry I can't be of help. Symbolism plays a very large part in voodoo, as in other religions. If there were other objects on the altar, they could help explain what my photograph was doing there."

I opened the manila envelope I had brought with me, took out the two photographs, handed him the head-and-shoulders shot. "This is a copy of your photo."

He made a soft hissing sound. "It looks like an army surveillance photo."

"And this is how it was displayed on the altar."

Fournier studied the second photograph for a few moments, then smiled thinly as he slowly nodded his head. "Yes," he said, handing me back the pictures, "this explains it. Very interesting."

"It means something to you?"

"This is what's called an array of atonement. Apparently your murderer and torturer was truly sorry for the crimes he had committed. He was seeking forgiveness. That's the meaning of the cross, voodoo fetishes, and *vèvès* on the altar. My photograph almost certainly represents a symbol of how he felt he should have behaved during his lifetime. He may also have been praying to me for intercession with God, as a Catholic does to a saint. That's unclear. What is clear is his regret for past misdeeds and his desire for redemption. That's probably why he agreed to cooperate with you in the first place. It's a shame he was killed before you could talk to him. I believe you would have found him most cooperative."

"It certainly is a shame," I said, replacing the photographs, rising to my feet, and extending my hand. "But at least you've satisfied my curiosity. Thank you for your time, Professor."

Fournier stood up, shook my hand. "I'm sorry I can't be of help to you in tying the CIA to what went on over there for decades."

So was I. "It's all right, Professor. The fact that you're willing to testify to what you did see going on could prove very helpful."

"I can provide a good deal of information on corruption within the Church in Haiti, and the collaboration of the Church hierarchy with the ruling class. I'll be happy to write it all down for you."

"Thanks, but I think we'll leave the Church out of this one. We've got enough other things to do that are more important than getting into a spitting contest with Rome. Thanks again."

*I used a pay phone to call Carl* Beauvil in Spring Valley to tell him what I had learned about Dr. Guy Fournier and the photograph; I didn't see how the information could be of any use to him, but his willingness to help us deserved appropriate payback. Then I headed over to the Federal Building to see if some long-overdue documents we had requested under the Freedom of Information Act had arrived. They hadn't. Since I was out of the house anyway, I decided to catch up on some background research I'd been putting off, so I headed uptown to the public library at Forty-second Street.

It was late afternoon when I got back to the brownstone. Garth was hard at work hacking away at the computer in my office. He was still using only his index fingers, but he started wriggling the other digits when he looked up and saw me. "How'd it go?"

"Total waste of time. It seems the general was feeling a little guilty about all the people he'd castrated and blinded, and he was using Fournier's picture to try to pray his way into voodoo heaven."

Garth grunted. "Somehow I doubt he made it."

"Somehow I agree."

There was a knock on the door, and I turned as Francisco entered the office. The bright floral print tie he was wearing with his gray three-piece suit clashed with the somber expression on his face. "You've been gone much longer than expected, sir."

"Yeah, well, I had a couple of errands to—"

"The protocol we established at the beginning of this investigation calls for the both of you to leave an anticipated daily schedule with me, and then if either you, Garth, or the two of you together are going to be away longer than expected, you call the office. If I'm not here, you leave a message on the office machine."

I looked over at Garth. "Were you worried?"

Garth pretended to think about it for a few moments, then said, "Not really."

Francisco was not amused. "I still think we should stick to the protocol, sir. You didn't check in the other night either. I have responsibilities. The protocol was set up when you accepted this assignment because it was agreed that the two of you could be in constant danger. If I think anything may have happened to the two of you, I'm to contact Veil immediately, and he'll provide for my personal safety while I deliver the work you've completed to the senator, with copies to the police and FBI. I almost did exactly that the night the two of you spent in the Spring Valley police station. For all I knew, you could both have been dead. I'm not being overly protective, sir. Considering the nature of the enemy, this is just good business practice. It was your idea."

"You're right, Francisco," I said seriously. "Garth and I have both been a bit forgetful. We'll try to improve our performance in the future."

"Thank you, sir," Francisco replied, and smiled. "I have a return address for the plagiarist, sir."

"Already?"

He shrugged. "It wasn't rocket science, sir. I didn't think it would be that difficult, so I didn't bother to hire a temp. A number of the editors I spoke with were familiar with Mr. Dickens' work, and they were all sympathetic. One of them had just received a submission from this Jefferson Kelly, so she still had the stamped, self-addressed return envelope that came with it. The address is in Huntsville, Alabama. I got a telephone number and called. It's the home district office of William P. Kranes."

Garth had resumed typing, but now he paused and looked up from the computer. *"The* William P. Kranes?"

Francisco nodded. "Yes, Garth. That one. The new Speaker of the House of Representatives."

Garth and I looked at each other, and my brother raised his eyebrows slightly. "Interesting development," he said quietly.

Indeed it was. Representative William P. Kranes was a pudgy, gremlin-like figure with a head of bushy brown hair and elfin smile, one of several ultra-conservative, howling junkyard dogs of C-SPAN who'd become leader of the pack, surfing to power in the last election on the crest of a powerful wave he'd been instrumental in creating, a poisonous, rushing tsunami of homophobia, antifeminism, and an entire devil's thesaurus of hysterical code words intended to give aid and comfort to anybody who was antiblack, antipoor, anti-anything that wasn't basically white, middle-class, and male. He was the most powerful man in Congress, now third in line of succession to the presidency, but only one of several southerners who now sat in key positions of power. Much to the dismay of both Garth and myself, it seemed to us that in the last election the Confederacy had finally won the last, great battle of the War Between the States, demonstrating without question that what a majority of Americans wanted to be— for a while, at least—was part of a nation of antebellum southerners in a time and place when states' rights ruled and "people of color," immigrants, women, homosexuals, and virtually every other minority group "knew their place," which was at the back of the bus, or even under it. Garth had been only half joking when he'd remarked one day that it could only be a matter of time before lynching was legalized as part of some new "Law and Order" package.

"Nice job, Francisco," I said. "Now you can go back to your other work."

"Yes, sir," Francisco replied, and left to return to his office at the front.

"So," I said, walking over to Garth, "the situation is not without its irony. It turns out that one of William P. Kranes's racist, fascist flunkies is our copycat. Wouldn't he be surprised to learn whose work he's been stealing and claiming as his own? I think it's funny as hell."

I knew Garth thought it was funny too, but he wasn't smiling. "I'd pay good money to be able to set up and watch a meeting between Moby Dickens and his admirer."

"And I'd double it. But you know it isn't going to happen. Delivering the bad news to Mr. Kelly is part of our job."

Garth nodded. "It could also be a woman, someone using 'Jefferson Kelly' as a pseudonym. Kranes is a big shot and that's a big district to service. Even so, how many people can he have working there, with access to office mail? It shouldn't be that hard to dig him—or her—out. He's probably wearing a T-shirt with 'I Am a Poet' written on it."

"One of us can pop down there and have a chat with Mr. Kelly after we finish the report."

Garth shook his head. "It won't wait. Unfinished business is a distraction we don't need."

"Unfinished business. You're joking, right?"

"No," Garth replied evenly, fixing me with his steady gaze. "I thought I'd explained to you—in detail—the metaphysics of this thing. Taking care of Mr. Dickens' problem is ultimately more important than trying to cure America of the CIA. In the end, all we're probably going to get from the CIA investigation is a lot of grief, frustration, booing, and hissing. But with this, we help Moby Dickens get his soul back. Think about it."

"I am thinking about it. It'll wait two and a half weeks."

"No. It won't."

"Squirrelly, Garth. Very squirrelly."

My brother didn't smile. Finally I rolled my eyes, slapped my fore-head, and continued. *"Jesus!* I'll send Francisco."

"No good. One of us has to go. Somebody has to read this Kelly the riot act, and Francisco's not the one to do that."

"Reading people the riot act is your department. If you think it's so important to do this now, then *you* go. Metaphysically speaking, that seems the right course of action."

Garth again shook his head. "Still no good. Kranes is a big bag of pus; every time he opens his mouth, something poisonous pops out. I might run into him there. If I lay eyes on the fat, hypocritical, dem-agogue fascist son of a bitch, I might tear his head off."

"Congress is in special session, which means Kranes is almost certainly in Washington. And if he's not there, he's off someplace with his forces of darkness planning for their party's convention. You won't run into him."

"Well, I have to assume that anybody working for him is also a bag of pus. I don't trust myself. This requires a deft hand, Mongo. It's best that you go."

"Garth, stop jerking me around! I went to see Fournier, so it's your turn to go on the fucking metaphysical road. Considering the way you chug along on that computer, we'll waste a whole day if I go."

"The report will get done on time." Garth paused, leaned back in my chair, and smiled slyly. "We'll flip a coin."

"I always lose coin tosses with you."

"Maybe this time it will be different."

It wasn't.

# CHAPTER 6

*I*'d brought my laptop computer along with me in order to get some work done on my early-morning flight to Huntsville, but instead I found myself reading through more of the collected works of Thomas Dickens that I'd brought with me. The more of his poetry I read, the more I understood Moby Dickens' desire for anonymity. All of the poems were beautifully crafted, capturing the essence of feeling in the sparest of words. All were perceptive, some startlingly so. Some were funny, others achingly sad. In a sense, all of his poems were about prisons—but not those of concrete and steel. Dickens' subject was the many different kinds of prisons we construct for ourselves and share with our cobuilders, those that are built for us and which we are thrown into, and, finally, those we inhabit alone. Moby Dickens' prison now was his body—ugly, tattooed, and menacing—and his greatest fear was that readers who saw him would never again be able to look beyond the shadows and bars of his flesh to see the pure fire of the artist within; the imagined echoes of steel clanging on steel would drown out the gentle and beautiful songs he sang. It made me sad to think about it. Reading the man's poems, often seeing an image of the poet's face superimposed on the pages, I even stopped thinking about the CIA, its voodoo hit squad, and the mutilation and death they left in their wake.

It was all enough to make me start taking some of my mysteriously bent brother's points more seriously. I even considered the possibility that maybe he wasn't being as obsessive and nutty about the plagiarism business as I'd first thought. I might even tell him that when I got back, although I doubted it.

I took a cab from the airport into town, to the three-story, glass-faced building which housed William P. Kranes's congressional district offices. I didn't know how much space in the building Kranes used, but I strongly suspected it might be all of it. Lots of staff, phone-answerers, clerical workers, home-based political operatives, political cronies and friends of political cronies. If Jefferson Kelly was a pseudonym, and its user was serious about not wanting his or her real identity known, rooting that person out could turn out to be one slow horse of a job, and I was determined to be back in New York that night. If I couldn't find Jefferson Kelly by the end of office hours, Garth was just going to have to sit on his metaphysics for two and a half weeks, or come down here himself.

I needn't have worried.

The secretary commanding the large, brightly lighted reception area was a buxom woman with the reddest hair I'd ever seen, and crimson lipstick to match. Her flawless skin was like alabaster, and her eyes really were the color of robins' eggs. The sight of her was almost enough to make me reconsider a lot of my antisouthern prejudices and start humming "Dixie." On a beige plastic panel directly behind her was a very large poster on which a poem entitled "Prison Walls" was written in flowing, hand-lettered calligraphy. It was almost an exact copy of Moby Dickens' "Razor Wire," which I'd read on the plane. This one was signed by Jefferson Kelly.

"Oh, you're so *cute*," the redhead giggled as I approached her desk.

Ah. A remark that in New York would have elicited from me an acidic, withering retort here, down in the land of cotton, squeezed from me a goofy smile and a gooey, "Why, thank you, ma'am."

"How can I help you, Mister . . . ?"

"Dickens. Thomas Dickens." I pointed to the poster behind her. "I'm a big fan of Jefferson Kelly. I see you are too. I'm always searching in the poetry journals for his work. I'm even seriously considering starting a fan club. Good poets are an endangered species, along with people who can appreciate their work."

The woman grinned, revealing a set of teeth as even, white, and shining as an ivory highway to heaven. She turned around in her chair to admire the poster, then turned back to me and leaned forward on her desk. Her smile had turned conspiratorial, and she whispered, "Do you know who Jefferson Kelly really is?"

"Jefferson Kelly isn't Jefferson Kelly?"

"It's Speaker *Kranes!*" she gushed, then opened her eyes wide, covered her mouth with her hand and quickly looked around, acting as if she had just given away some state secret.

I put my hands on my hips, cocked my head to one side, and clucked my tongue. *"No!"*

"Yes!" she said, lowering her voice to about the level of a stage whisper. "Isn't he *wonderful?* He's *so* talented! But he's also very modest. He won't use his real name because he's afraid editors would only publish his poetry because of who he is. Also, I think he's kind of embarrassed by all his talent. Only a few people know—his family, friends, and a few people in town. And now you know; you were so enthusiastic, I just couldn't stop myself from sharing that with you."

"Well, I'll be doggoned," I said, shaking my head in awe and wonder. "Boy, I'd sure like to meet the man. As a matter of fact, Jefferson Kelly—Speaker Kranes, that is—is the reason I stopped in. I don't remember where I heard it, but somebody told me Jefferson Kelly worked for Speaker Kranes, here in his district office. I'm in town on business, so I thought I'd pop in to tell him how much I enjoy his work, and maybe get to shake his hand. Now it looks as if it will have to wait until I get to Washington."

"Actually, the Speaker is in town for a couple of days. He's in his office now, but I'm afraid he doesn't have time to see you, even for a minute or two. His appointment schedule is just jam-packed from morning to night, and he's already an hour behind."

"So near to the great man and yet so far. What a crushing disappointment."

"I understand how you feel. But I doubt you'll have much better luck in Washington, Mr. Dickens. You know what a very busy man he is now all the time." She paused, again flashed her divine smile. "He's leading a revolution, changing the country."

"Oh, don't I know it. But why don't we give it a try anyway? Give Che Guevara a buzz on the intercom and tell him Thomas Dickens is here to discuss poetry with him. Maybe he'll also think I'm cute."

She turned serious. "Oh, I can't disturb him when he's in conference, Mr. Dickens. If you'd like, I'll try to get him to sign a copy of one of his poems, and I'll send it to you. I'm sure he'll be pleased by your interest."

I turned serious. "Thomas Dickens, missy," I said, pointing to the twenty-button intercom beside her elbow. "Guaranteed that he's going to want to talk to me, probably immediately. Also guaranteed that he's going to be extremely displeased if I walk out of here and he finds out later that I was here and you didn't notify him. He's going to be so disturbed that he'll probably cancel all of his appointments for the rest of the day, and then he'll probably fire you. Better not take a chance."

The redhead with the shiny crimson lips stared at me strangely for a few moments, then tentatively reached over and pressed the top button on her intercom.

"What is it, Jane?" a man's irritated voice asked tersely.

"Sir, I'm very sorry to disturb you," the woman said quickly, looking at me with both annoyance and nervousness. "There's a gentleman by the name of Thomas Dickens out here, and he insists you'll want to speak with him. Should I call security?"

"Who?"

She repeated the name very slowly. "Thom-as Dick-ens."

There was a considerable pause, and then a strained, "Give me five minutes, then send him in."

I stood at the desk, alternately smiling at the woman and glancing toward a gray-suited, stern-faced man wearing dark glasses whom I assumed was a Secret Service agent assigned to Kranes because of the congressman's newfound place in the line of succession to the presidency. He had appeared out of nowhere, and was standing a few feet away off to my left. Two minutes later a heavy, carved oak door to my right opened and a tall man carrying a briefcase and wearing a Stetson and cowboy boots with his black, pin-striped suit came stalking out, obviously in a huff because his audience with the king of the Hill had been abbreviated. I gave Kranes three more minutes to compose himself, then walked unbidden through the door and into a large, plushly furnished office decorated with expensive, mounted shotguns and photographs of Kranes with enough politicians, sports and movie stars, and world leaders to populate a small town.

Kranes was sitting hunched over his desk and trying to look busy as he scribbled furiously on a yellow legal pad. His bushy brown hair was unkempt, as if he had recently been nervously running a hand through it, and the little I could see of his forehead and face was flushed. Unlike most people, Kranes looked even fatter in person than on television, and I wondered if he ever now regretted the venomous comments he used to make about his opponents' less attractive physical characteristics when he had been a younger, less powerful, and much thinner man. I somehow doubted it.

Kranes, whose heart I assumed was racing along at a pretty good clip at the moment, was a man who had proudly declared that he was going to take the country back to the 1950s, when "things were the way they're supposed to be." A lot of people, including myself, believed that the time he had in mind for the country was a few centuries further back than that. In one of his many unguarded moments, during one of his many histrionic rambles on C-SPAN before his party had ascended to power, he had described slavery as "not all bad, an economic system dictated by market forces, and a kind of health-care and welfare system for the underprivileged." He was a piece of work. It was because of Kranes that a lot of people, including not a few conservatives, prayed every day for the health of the president and vice president, as liberal as they were. Kranes was occasionally touted as a presidential candidate himself, but I doubted that was a serious possibility. His party was most pleased to have installed him as Speaker of the House of Representatives, but the only popular elections he had ever won had been to his seat in Congress representing this district in Alabama; with his spacey views and his willingness to express them, I considered it highly unlikely he could ever win even a statewide, much less national, election, even considering the sour mood the country was in. Garth would laugh and call me a naive fool, arguing that William P. Kranes was as all-American as apple pie.

Finally, having apparently decided upon some kind of strategy for dealing with the man whose poetry he had been plagiarizing, Kranes looked up. I was spared the boyish, toothy grin he liked to flash at the unwary; his eyes went wide, his mouth dropped open, and he snapped back in his chair as if he had been goosed with a cattle prod. His face, which had been red before, now went white. His features rapidly morphed into a variety of expressions, ending with one that looked curiously like relief.

"Your name isn't Dickens!" he triumphantly announced, rising from his chair and pointing a trembling, accusatory index finger in my direction, reminding me of nothing so much as an overweight edition of the other Dickens' Christmas Past. "You're that Frederickson dwarf! I'm on the Intelligence Committee, and I know all about what you and that ultra-liberal president and all your hippie friends are up to! If you think you're going to interview me as part of your effort to gut the CIA, you've got another think coming! Hell will freeze over first! I want you the hell out of my office!"

"Mr. Speaker," I said, smiling sweetly. "The Frederickson dwarf is not here to interview you about the CIA. You wouldn't tell me anything I want to know, even if you knew anything I want to know, which you probably don't, since you and the other members of the intelligence committees in both the House and Senate are usually the last to know about anything really important going on in the intelligence community. What you people hear is all honey and bullshit."

The relief, if it had been that, I had glimpsed on his face and in his brown eyes suddenly vanished, and now Speaker of the House of Representatives William P. Kranes looked more than a bit haunted. "What do you want, then?" he asked tightly.

"Thomas Dickens. You think I pulled that name out of a hat? It's the reason you agreed to squeeze me into your frantic schedule."

Kranes slowly sank back down into his chair, looked away toward a shotgun mounted in a glass case. "The name does sound vaguely familiar," he said quietly, "but I can't place it."

"No? Let's see if I can't jog your memory." I reached into my brief-case, removed a sheaf of Moby Dickens' poems, and tossed them on the other man's desk, right under his nose. "Why don't you read over these poems by Mr. Dickens and then see if you can't remember where you first saw the name? If that doesn't help, I have some other poems in here with *your* name on them that might help."

There was a long pause, and then I saw his gaze flick away from the shotgun down to the papers scattered over his desk. He swallowed hard, then said softly, "This is, uh, very . . ."

"I think 'embarrassing' is the word you're searching for. Your career as a poet is toast, Mr. Speaker. Now, do you want to discuss this in a reasonable manner, or do you want to keep on embarrassing yourself?"

"Sit down, Frederickson," he said in the same quiet, slightly choked tone.

I sat, moving the chair back a couple of feet so that I had a clear view of his face over the top of the desk. "Have you plagiarized anyone else's poems?"

He slowly shook his head.

"So you're selective, and you've got taste. But why'd you do it? If you've got the heart to appreciate Dickens' poetry, why not write your own?"

He breathed deeply, slowly shook his head again. His lips were compressed tightly, and there were spots of color high on his chubby cheeks, but he now held his head erect and looked me squarely in the eye. "I, uh . . . I don't even think I was aware I was doing it, if you want the truth. I used to be an English professor, you know. I taught poetry, and I still read an enormous amount of it in my limited spare time."

"Obviously. It seems what you don't do is write any of your own. You steal somebody else's."

The color in his cheeks spread across his face and up onto his forehead, but he kept his composure, and his voice remained steady as he continued to meet my gaze. "I've admired Mr. Dickens' poetry from the time it first started appearing in various journals. I think what must have happened is that I read so much of it, so often, that I just started to think of them as poems I'd written. Can you understand that?"

"What a load of horseshit."

"People don't usually talk to me like that, Frederickson!"

"Horseshit, horseshit, double horseshit. Other people don't know about this little character flaw of yours. You used another man's work to impress your family, friends, and local constituents. You used Thomas Dickens' poems to present yourself as something you're not, an artist. This business has jogged *my* memory, and I now recall a television interview a few years back that one of your campaign workers gave to CNN in which she waxed eloquent about how she wished other people could only know about this artistic dimension of yours, how you were an accomplished poet who was too modest to write under your own name. At *that* time, I dismissed it as horseshit. It's still horseshit, but it comes from a different horse altogether."

"I meant no harm!"

"You harmed Thomas Dickens."

"How? There's no money in writing poetry. And I always submitted my . . . interpretations . . . to magazines that had considerably less prestige and circulation than the journals in which they'd originally appeared. Do you know how few people *read* those magazines? A *handful*. These are *literary* journals, for Christ's sake! They're read mostly by college professors and students, a few poetry buffs, and a few hundred poet wannabes—like me, yes! But I never made a penny! Most of the magazines I submitted to are cranked out in somebody's basement and distributed to a couple of hundred people at most. So where's the harm?"

"My brother handles metaphysics."

"What? What the hell are you talking about?"

Kranes wasn't getting it—as I hadn't gotten it at first. I thought about the problem, reluctantly made a decision. I was decidedly uncomfortable with what I was about to do, but thought it might be necessary to impress upon the man behind the desk the seriousness of the situation—what was at stake for Moby Dickens, and for him. I asked, "You know anything about Dickens?"

"Not personally, no."

"Neither does anyone else, and that's the way he wants to keep it; that's why he hired me to come and have this little talk with you. But I'm going to tell you a few things about him anyway. Thomas Dickens isn't exactly poor, because he has a steady union job working for the New York Sanitation Department, but he comes from a background of poverty."

Kranes's brown eyes widened slightly, and he slowly blinked. "-He's a *garbageman?*"

"Uh-huh. And it gets better. He's a black ex-convict who served a lengthy prison term for an act of self-defense that was called murder. The reason I'm telling you this is because you can't exactly be described as a friend of the poor, black, or convicts—ex or otherwise. If you had your way, people like Thomas Dickens would be summarily executed the week after they were convicted. He's a member of three different minority groups of people you've stereotyped and demonized as undeserving, stupid, lazy folks who bloat the prisons and the welfare rolls. Putting these people down is how you keep getting reelected down here in your district, and it's the underlying message that won your party the last national election. Now it turns out that you've been bloating your own ego and reputation by stealing the intellectual goods of a black ex-convict who comes from a poor southern background. You have some wealth, family, reputation, fame, and great power. Mr. Dickens has none of these things; all he has are his words, and you've been stealing them from him. You've harmed Mr. Dickens because you've appropriated everything that means anything to him."

The color drained from Kranes's face, and his eyes in his pudgy face suddenly glinted with anger. "You've come here to try to blackmail me!"

"I've come here to ask you to stop plagiarizing Mr. Dickens' work—or anyone else's, for that matter. If you want to be thought of as a poet, write your own poems."

"What does Dickens want?"

I shook my head. "I could have sworn I just told you. He wants you to stop copying his fucking poems. Get it?"

Kranes sucked in a deep breath, slowly let it out. "That's all? He's not going to attempt to . . . embarrass me?"

"How you could possibly be embarrassed more by this than by all the crap that comes out of your mouth every day is totally beyond me, but I'm not one of your fans. Dickens doesn't even know who you are, and if he did know he wouldn't care. The man's a poet, and all he cares about are his words. He doesn't want money from you. *I*, on the other hand, think it would be appropriate for you to pay Mr. Dickens an honorarium of, say, five hundred dollars. We'll call it a fee for your past leasing of his work. Those poems you claimed as your own may even have gotten you some swing votes among the not-so-conservatives around here who took them to mean that you're really a sensitive guy at heart who doesn't mean all those nasty things he says. Hey, maybe it's true. Don't think that I'm unimpressed by the fact that you picked Thomas Dickens' work to copy. It spoke to and touched you, which may very well mean that you routinely put your brain in park and let your mouth do all the work, pandering to people's ignorance, gullibility, and prejudices simply in order to stay in power. Maybe the politician in you killed off the rest of the man."

"That's enough, Frederickson. For five hundred dollars, I shouldn't have to sit here and listen to your liberal bullshit. The country doesn't agree with you. Your time is past."

"Make the check out to Thomas Dickens. I'll take it with me, along with your written statement acknowledging your plagiarism and pledging to cease and desist. That goes no further than my confidential files. You'll also pay my fee and expenses. I'll send you an itemized bill after I figure out how much time my staff and I have spent on this matter."

"No check for Dickens. I'll give you cash."

"Whatever you like. I'll give you a receipt."

"I don't want a receipt. I'll pay your fee and expenses, but make sure that the bill you send me makes no mention of Thomas Dickens or any plagiarized poetry. Just bill me for general expenses. And no letter. I've told you I meant no harm, and I'm telling you I won't do it again."

I studied him for a few moments, then nodded my head. "All right, Mr. Speaker. I'll take your word for it."

He pushed his chair back, took a key from his vest pocket, leaned over, and opened a locked drawer in his desk. When he straightened up he was holding a fistful of cash. He counted out five hundred dollars and put the bills in a plain envelope that he tossed across the desk to me. "And I have your word that this is the end of it?" he asked in an even tone.

"As far as I'm concerned, yes. I can't speak for Mr. Dickens, and he's the injured party. I have an obligation to tell him who Jefferson Kelly is—but only if he asks, which I'm not even sure he'll do. I won't volunteer the information. I wouldn't lose any sleep over it. He's not interested in you. I'm not even certain he'll accept your money; if he doesn't, I'll send you a check along with my bill."

I put the cash in my briefcase, rose, and turned toward the door.

"Hey," Kranes said quietly.

I turned back. "Hey what?"

"What you're doing is wrong. It's just incredibly wrong-headed and short-sighted, even for an ultra-liberal like yourself."

"Trying to protect a man's intellectual property?"

"Working to destroy the CIA."

"Did you say 'destroy'? From your mouth to God's ears."

"The KGB hasn't been disbanded, you know. They've just been regrouped into an organization with a different name. They're just as powerful and evil as they ever were. Russia is bound to return to totalitarianism, and they will once again be the number-one threat to this nation and to world peace."

"Are you trying to appeal to my patriotism, Mr. Speaker?"

"And if I am?" he asked in the same quiet tone. "Is 'Patriotism' such a dirty word to you?"

"In some mouths, yes. It's a weapon-word, and too often it's used to try to shout down other people. It's a word that kills. Patriotism is just another form of religion, and like all religion it's bad for the individual and frequently deadly to the people around him. Incidentally, I've been hunted, shot at, and tortured by the KGB on a goodly number of occasions, so you can keep that bogeyman in your closet. I know the monster a hell of a lot better than you do."

"You're an atheist, aren't you?"

"My mother taught me never to discuss sex, religion, or politics in polite company. Let's just say that if I had my way, every single so-called 'house of worship' on the planet would be outfitted with a sign warning that 'the creationist and exclusionary fantasies for sale in this establishment are hazardous to your health and the health of others.'"

"So you don't love God. How can you live without God?"

"How can you live *with* God? I'll admit it can sometimes be a bitch taking responsibility for your own actions, and holding other people accountable for theirs, but I *still* don't understand how you can live with the chauvinistic, ill-tempered, stand-up comedian so many humans call God. It truly is a mystery to me. If I did believe in this deity, I'd be a guerrilla fighter looking for a suitable replacement. I mean, your guy is worse than useless; he's arbitrary."

"And you have no love for this country?"

"I don't believe countries should be loved or hated; they should constantly be improved by the people who live within their borders, and especially by their leaders. People like you. You asked me if I loved this geographical entity called the United States. I'll ask you if you really think you're improving it by all the divisive things you say and do. If I'm even half right, if much of what comes out of your mouth is posturing and tap dancing to stay in office collecting a government paycheck and accumulating ever greater power, is that patriotism?"

To my surprise, he did not reply. To my even greater surprise, I found myself giving him points for the honesty of his silence. To my utter astonishment, in that moment I felt a kind of bonding with the man, if not much affection.

"I believe the United States to be the most diverse and complex society on earth, Mr. Speaker," I continued quietly. "Anybody who tries to wrap his mind around the whole thing just gets brain sprain. Nobody should say they understand this country."

"I say I understand this country, Frederickson. And I do love this country with all my heart. There's something wrong with a man who doesn't love his country."

"Yeah, but people like you would feel exactly the same way about Russia if that's where you'd been born; that's *religion,* not rationality. I find the United States to be a relatively safe, comfortable, and pleasurable place in which to live and go about my business. This society allows me to create my own country, if you will, and I'm grateful for that. I want to keep it that way, for myself and for others. But sometimes you have to snip out a few tumors if you want to keep a body healthy."

"We need the CIA, Frederickson. Who's going to protect you— protect all of us—when the KGB is in ascendancy again?"

"Hopefully, a responsible and professional intelligence service that isn't run like an old boys' social club and that doesn't spend decades seriously exaggerating the strength of the enemy in order to feather their nest and fill their rice bowl. That's what the CIA has done."

"The world is still a very dangerous place, Frederickson."

"Made more dangerous by those Ops lads in Langley. This country spends upwards of forty-eight billion dollars a year on its intel— "

"Where did you get that number? It's classified."

"Spare me. The key word in Central Intelligence Agency is *central*. The director is supposed to coordinate the activities of the dozen other intelligence agencies, from the military to the State Department. That's a good idea. But the CIA doesn't want to supervise and coordinate the show; they insist on *being* the show. You've got lunatics in Ops over there. I know that because I've also been hunted, shot at, and tortured by the CIA. The KGB is the Russians' problem; the CIA is ours. I'm just trying to do my part to solve that problem."

"You grossly exaggerate the allegedly illegal or harmful acts of the CIA. You have a personal agenda."

"You bet I do. If you ever have a couple of days to spare and are interested in *really* being briefed on some of the stunts those Ops people have pulled, I'll be happy to oblige you."

"You're wasting your time, you know," Kranes said tersely. "Nothing is going to happen to the CIA. There's almost certain to be a change of administrations in the next election, and the new president isn't likely to act on a single one of any of the recommendations you people make."

"I suspect you're at least half right. But the report will be out there, and don't be so sure nothing is going to happen. If the report is sound, and it will be, and the CIA's misbehavior has been egregious, which it has been, doing nothing in order to preserve the status quo will be an embarrassment to you and your party, not to the commission. I'm not talking romantic Cold War cloak-and-dagger skulduggery here, Kranes; this is about serious criminal activity."

"Diversion of funds from arms sales? Old news. Most of the country applauds what the CIA did in that situation. The goal was righteous."

"Yeah, well, let's see how hard people clap when they find out that the company has been systematically funneling bundles of money into the coffers of right-wing PACs in this country. It may be common knowledge that they try to rig elections in other countries, but I think not a few people are going to be surprised to find out that they try to do the same thing right here on American soil. As a matter of fact, three-quarters of a million dollars that flowed to your very own Get-Back organization was given to you by the CIA."

"That's a lie!" Kranes snapped, leaping to his feet. "Are you accusing me of—"

"Sit down and relax, Mr. Speaker. I'm not accusing you of anything. Neither you nor any of your money managers knew where the money really came from. Then again, you often go out of your way not to look *too* closely at some of your financial benefactors, but that's a different discussion. The three-quarter mil was carefully laundered—just not carefully enough. The CIA doesn't go around writing 'CIA' on its checks. Does the name Pluto Products ring a bell? They contributed the money. But that company doesn't make any products, Plutonic or otherwise. It's a CIA front, a shell that formally had headquarters in Haiti. That one we can prove. You see, the lads and lassies of Langley make every effort to use and manipulate certain politicians in this country the same as you use and manipulate people. There's a certain irony in that, don't you think?"

Kranes, red-faced, didn't sit, and he didn't relax. Instead he balled up his fists and leaned forward on his desk. "I've never taken any money from the CIA! It would be illegal for them to even offer it!"

"There you go."

"I still say it's a lie!"

"You'll be a better judge of that when the report is released. You can examine the data for yourself. Then we'll see if you're still so anxious to keep things just the way they are."

"You're not this country, Frederickson! *I'm* this country!"

"You're probably right, and so what? What does that have to do with the need to abolish, or at least drastically reorganize, the CIA? They're certainly not the country either."

"You're working for a bunch of disloyal and discredited ultra-liberal social engineers who still want to tear down this country and its institutions even after the American people have booted them out of office!"

"My, my. I do seem to have touched a nerve. You know, there's something missing in you people. I'm not sure what it is. It's not enough to call you mean-spirited, or hypocritical, or manipulative, or demagogic. It's more than that. First you ride to power by fanning hatred of the poor, blacks, immigrants, and just about everybody else who isn't white and middle-class. Then you work to actually throw all those people overboard. And now, here you are slobbering over the poor old CIA. What the hell's the matter with you?"

Kranes took a series of deep breaths, then slowly sat back down in his chair. "Our business is finished, Dr. Frederickson," he said evenly. "I expect you to keep your part of the bargain, which means I don't expect to hear from you or Thomas Dickens again. Now get out of my office."

I got out, called a taxi to take me to the airport. I was sorry I had wasted my time arguing politics with William P. Kranes, but I wasn't sorry I had flown down to Huntsville, and I wasn't sorry Garth and I had taken on the plagiarism case of Moby Dickens. I had Garth to

thank for that. In fact, I felt good—better than at any time since
Garth and I had received our invitation and marching orders from the
head of the commission and we had plunged headlong into the assignment. The fact of the matter was that I had considerably more affection for the United States of America than I ever would have let on
to William P. Kranes, for I believed he cheapened the currency of patriotism. I found America a truly remarkable nation, if for nothing
else than its resiliency and the fact that it could survive leaders like
Kranes. And I knew I was guilty of more than a little hypocrisy myself, and was not immune from little snits of self-righteousness. I'd
told myself that what Garth and I were doing was good for the country. I still believed that, but I hadn't been working out of a sense of
patriotism; for months I'd been running on a full head of adrenaline
primed by hatred. It hadn't been good for me, and only now, with the
peace and calm I was experiencing in the aftermath of this other, very
minor storm, did I realize that. Helping Moby Dickens had been a
truly righteous act, and I felt pleased with myself. I was ready to return to our report in a more relaxed frame of mind, and I was now
confident we would finish it with time to spare. Tracking down a plagiarist had proved purgative.

# CHAPTER 7

*I*t was a good thing that I was enjoying a personal buzz from the quick and successful completion of the poetry business, because it looked, at least from my point of view, as if the electorate was going to get a lot more than it had bargained for in the last election, and the country was going to sink even deeper into a right-wing malaise that could last for decades.

Three days after I'd returned from Huntsville, CNN reported that the Honorable Mabel Roscowicz, the only remaining liberal on the Supreme Court after the death of Richard Weiner, had died in her sleep, apparently the victim of a heart attack. Now the next president would have two Supreme Court vacancies to fill, which meant the Court was going to swing even further past the center, all the way over to the hard right. The ultra-conservatives currently in power, and the very conservative president likely to be elected, were going to leave behind quite a legacy, even if, at some time in the future, the voters began to have second thoughts about their stewardship. Depressing. And it was almost enough to make me forget Garth's little tutorial on the things that were important. Francisco's interruption didn't help.

"Sir?"

"What is it, Francisco?" I asked irritably, glancing up from my computer.

"I'm sorry to disturb you, sir, but there's somebody here who insists on seeing you. He doesn't have an appointment."

"Again? I must be living in sin."

"I told him you're very busy, but he won't take no for an answer. He claims it's extremely urgent."

"Fuck him," I said, turning back to my keyboard. "Let him sit out there as long as he wants. If he keeps disturbing you, have one of Veil's security people throw him out."

"It's Taylor Mackintosh, sir."

I typed in a line, stopped again, leaned back in my chair, and frowned at Francisco. *"The* Taylor Mackintosh?"

"Yes, sir. That Taylor Mackintosh."

"I thought he was dead."

"He looks alive to me, sir. He's waiting in the outer office."

"What the hell does he want?"

"He won't say, sir. He demands to talk to you."

I grunted, turned off the computer. "All right, send him in."

The old man who walked into my office was about five feet nine or ten, but he had always loomed larger on the screen—shot from low angles, or mounted on a horse, or with female leads who were always shorter than he was—in the movies I remembered from childhood and which still occasionally showed up on cable TV. Taylor Mackintosh had to be pushing eighty-five, but he was still obviously pretty spry. I'd heard rumors that he suffered from Alzheimer's disease, but his very pale blue eyes seemed clear and in focus as he glared at me from across the room. He was impeccably, if somewhat oddly, dressed in a gray, three-piece Armani suit with snakeskin cowboy boots. He wore a shirt that matched his eyes, and a black bolo tie with a turquoise clip. He looked and carried himself like, well—an old movie star. The only jarring note in his appearance was a cheap, impossibly ill-fitting and badly dyed toupee that made it look like he had a dead or sleeping muskrat on top of his head. A two-thousand-dollar suit and a muskrat toupee made me think that maybe the rumors about his diminished mental capacity were true. Either that, or he needed to hire himself a new dresser.

Taylor Mackintosh had to consider Charlton Heston, a younger man, his *bête noire*. Mackintosh had been the star of choice for virtually every biblical epic made—until Heston had come along. Mackintosh had played God on any number of occasions, but never Moses—and he was still known to harbor deep resentment over the fact that Heston had been chosen for that part. The irony was that Mackintosh, unlike Heston, was no friend of the arts. Dismissing his own career, he had, in his dotage, announced that the arts were for "lesbians and fairies," and did not ever deserve to be supported with a cent of taxpayers' money. Mackintosh also had a raging passion for guns, any gun, all guns of any size, shape, caliber, or color. He would dearly love to have been chosen as spokesman for the NRA, but again, Charlton Heston had gotten there first. He had comforted himself by agreeing to become TV-and-print spokesman for a tiny but very vocal band of gun lunatics that had thrown religion into the mix and which called themselves Guns for God and Jesus—or "Gingivitis," as they had affectionately been dubbed by certain members of the ultra-liberal media who didn't share their conviction that it was the God-given right of every man, woman, and child in America to own an Uzi and armor-piercing ammunition. Gingivitis was too nutty even for the NRA, which had been known to deny that the group even existed. I had no idea what Mackintosh could want with me.

"Good afternoon, sir," I said, rising and extending my hand. Age has its privileges, and Mackintosh's movies had given me hours of pleasure and much-needed escape from the pain and loneliness of my childhood in the single, shabby movie theater that still stood in my hometown in Peru County, Nebraska.

He marched across the office, stopped in front of my desk. Ignoring my outstretched hand, he reached into an inside pocket of his suit jacket and drew out a gold-plated fountain pen. "I'd just as soon skip the formalities, Frederickson," he said in a voice that had once been deep and resonant but was now raspy with age. "I'll give you my autograph, but I'm here to talk turkey."

I sat back down and motioned for him to pull up a chair. "I'll pass on the autograph, Mr. Mackintosh, but I'll be happy to listen to you gobble—as long as it doesn't take too long."

He didn't much like that, but it was hard for me to tell if he knew why he didn't like it. "I understand you're in possession of certain items that could prove damaging to a very good friend of mine."

I stared up into the angry, watery blue eyes and vaguely wondered if he was referring to the investigation of the CIA, or their Haiti connection. "I don't know what you're talking about, Mr. Mackintosh," I replied at last.

"You've got some so-called poems by some so-called Thomas Dickens."

Now there was a surprise. Mackintosh had not sat down, but was instead leaning on my desk and glowering down at me, so close I could smell his age and aftershave lotion. I stared back into the famous face for a few moments, then shook my head in disbelief and said, "Kranes *told* you about this?"

"What do you plan to do with these so-called poems?"

"Well, I hadn't planned—"

"Forget whatever you were about to say, because it would only be a lie. I know what you're planning to do, and I'm here to head you off at the pass. Nobody will believe you, but you could prove to be a nuisance. So I'm going to give you and your partner some nuisance money. Every man has his price, and I figure I have a pretty good idea what this business should be worth to you. So I'm going to make you an offer you can't refuse. It's better than you're going to get anywhere else, because the tabloids won't pay for a story about some stupid poems. One hundred and fifty thousand dollars. That's for the two of you."

It was the second time in three days I had gaped at somebody in awe and wonder, but this time my reaction wasn't feigned. The old man spoke gibberish in a patois of lines from old movie scripts. It suddenly struck me that Taylor Mackintosh was, indeed, quite insane, and I found myself feeling sorry for him. "Let's back up and waddle around the barnyard a little more slowly, Mr. Mackintosh," I said evenly. "You have to be very specific about what you think is a problem, and what you plan to do about it. I am not going to discuss any client's case with you. You have just this one second chance to get it right, because my time is limited. Now, take a deep breath and tell me why you're here."

He flushed, straightened up. "Bill Kranes is a good friend of mine. He's also one of the best men this country has ever produced. You and your liberal pals have cooked up some half-baked scheme to make him look bad just because he's written and published some poetry. You found out he used a pen name, and so you went out and found some black ex-convict to say he actually wrote them, and that Bill copied his work. Then you phonied up some old poetry magazines to back you up. You're planning to try to embarrass him and damage his reputation with this story."

"Your good friend Bill told you this?"

"He didn't have to. I'm not as naive as some people in this country, and I know what you're up to. I don't care what proof you say you have; I know this Thomas Dickens didn't write those poems of Bill's."

"And just what makes you so sure of that, Mr. Mackintosh?"

"Anybody with a lick of sense knows niggers can't write good poetry."

Ah. There went the last traces of my sympathy for the aged movie star with the bad toupee, and I wondered how much different his views could have been even before plaque had begun seizing up his brain cells. His statement left me not quite speechless. I sighed, shook my head, and said, "You are a clever old fox to figure that out."

"This man's a hero, Frederickson. The country is just starting to get on the right track after you liberals damn near destroyed it. The country needs his leadership, and friends of his are not going to stand idly by while people like you try to sully his name."

"You talk like he's going to run for president. Wouldn't that be a hoot."

"Two hundred thousand dollars, Frederickson. That's the absolute limit of what a group of people I represent are prepared to offer you to make this business go away. In return, you and your nigger partner will declare in writing that this slander about Bill copying the poems isn't true, and you pledge not to try to smear Bill, whether or not he decides to campaign for the presidency. Have we got a deal? You write up the letter, and I'll cut you a check right now."

"Don't you think I should consult with my partner in crime?"

"What nigger garbageman is going to turn down a hundred grand? You can probably give him ten or fifteen, and he'll be happy as a pig in shit. You can keep the rest for yourself."

Try as hard as I might, I just couldn't work up any kind of real mad at Taylor Mackintosh; the famous movie star was now just a deranged old man who had lived long enough to make a total fool out of himself. What I found profoundly puzzling was the question of why William P. Kranes would confide in such a man, one who could prove profoundly embarrassing to Kranes as well as to himself. If Kranes didn't trust me and wanted to risk blowing himself out of the water by using somebody like Mackintosh as a front man, that was his business, but I wasn't going to be any part of it. And I was going to con-

tinue to try to shield my satisfied client, who had never even asked if
Jefferson Kelly was the plagiarist's real name, and who had indeed
refused the "honorarium," which had been returned to Kranes by
certified check, along with my bill.

"Look, Mr. Mackintosh," I said quietly. "You've wandered onto
the wrong movie set here. The script you think you're following just
doesn't exist. There's no plot to embarrass or smear anyone. The
problem you're referring to, if there ever was such a problem, has
been successfully resolved."

"You expect me to believe that? Do I look like a fool?"

"I don't give turkey shit what you believe," I replied, my patience
beginning to wear a bit thin, "and what you look like is between you
and your mirror. For the life of me, I can't understand why your good
friend Bill discussed this with you—he must be even stupider than I
thought. But I will guarantee you this: he will *not* want you discussing
this with anyone else, and he won't be your good friend much longer
if you do. You should just forget the whole thing. That's the only free
advice I'm giving out today."

"How much money do you want, dwarf?!"

"Cut!" I snapped, leaping up from my chair and jabbing a finger
in the direction of the door as I stifled an impulse to burst out laugh-
ing. "Get the fuck out of my office before I throw you out! You used
the *D* word!"

His head snapped back and he retreated a step, obviously startled.
I made a shuffling motion as if I was coming around from behind my
desk, and he scurried backward, almost tripping over his feet. When
he had reached the open door, he turned back, his seamed, leathery
face twisted into an ugly mask of rage. "I can destroy you, dwarf!"

"There's the *D* word again! Get!"

He got. I instructed Francisco not to even tell me the next time
somebody showed up wanting an audience, and I went back to work.

I worked through the lunch hour, then skipped downtown to pick up our Freedom of Information documents, which had finally arrived. About 80 percent of every single page was blacked out, which we had anticipated, and which was fine with me. Garth and I didn't have time to fully analyze the information anyway, and all those blacked-out pages were going to look good in an appendix; Congress could decide for itself how badly it wanted to find out what was hidden beneath all that inky darkness. I grabbed a hot dog and coffee from a Sabrett vendor, and had just finished eating when my beeper went off. It was Garth. I walked to a pay phone at the corner and called the office. Garth answered.

"Yo."

"Mongo," Garth said in a soft voice that was tinged with sadness. "Meet me at the southwest corner of the Sheep Meadow."

"What's up?"

"Moby's dead. Somebody blinded him, sliced off his tongue, and cut out his heart. Henry called me. The police found your card in his pocket, and they want to talk to us."

*Garth and I stood in silence at the* edge of a copse of trees in Central Park, just inside a drooping band of yellow police tape, staring at the mutilated body of Moby Dickens. There was no blood on the grass, which, considering all the brutal surgery that had been performed on him, meant he had been slaughtered elsewhere and his body dumped here, where it was certain to be discovered at dawn by some birder, walker, or jogger. Moby Dickens wasn't Haitian, probably didn't know much of anything about Haiti, and couldn't have cared less about the CIA. His murder was apparently intended to send a personal message. To us.

"Jesus, Garth," I said, my voice cracking as tears rolled down my cheeks. "I gave him up. I did exactly what he didn't want anybody to do, which was to identify and describe him. I gave up his name, race, and occupation. I betrayed a client, and I might as well have painted a target on his back."

"You didn't kill him, Mongo," Garth said, putting an arm around my shoulders and drawing me closer to him.

"Oh yes, I did," I sobbed.

"What you did was a judgment call. You told Kranes about him in order to drive home a point. I'd have done exactly the same thing if I'd gone down there."

"Garth, I'm going to find and kill the sons of bitches who did this."

"What's going on, guys?"

I quickly wiped my eyes and put on a pair of sunglasses I'd brought with me before I turned to Henry Stamp, the NYPD detective who'd called Garth. Stamp was a stubby man with a wrinkled face and expressive green eyes that had remained burnished with kindness despite twenty-five years with the police, and all the things he had seen during that time. He was a good man, and both Garth and I liked him very much.

"His name is Thomas Dickens," I said to the detective in a voice that still cracked slightly. I cleared my throat. "He's a poet."

Henry Stamp turned to look at the naked, mutilated, heavily tattooed body lying on the grass at the edge of the trees. "A poet," he repeated in a flat tone.

"He also worked for the Sanitation Department. He's got an apartment down in the East Village."

"We know his name and address, Mongo. It was in his wallet, along with seventy-three bucks in cash. Your business card was in his pocket, and we were hoping you could shed some light. Obviously, robbery wasn't the motive. Somebody really took their time and did a number on this guy, then dumped him here. We're still looking, but we haven't found his heart. Whoever took it out must have left it where they killed him."

"They took it with them."

"How do you know that?"

"We've seen this kind of killing before. This is the seventh victim of a kind of voodoo hit squad that's been operating across the country for the past few months. I know how this will thrill you, but the FBI is going to want to know about this right away. You should call them first chance you get."

The detective had been writing in his notebook. Now he stopped, looked at me. "Jesus, I hate the FBIs."

"Yeah, well," I said, choking back a sob, "into each life a little rain must fall. You'll be working with them on this."

"You care to elaborate a bit for me, Mongo? There have been six other killings just like this one?"

I nodded, swallowed hard. The sun was hot on the back of my neck, and my mouth was very dry. I looked away from the body. "Garth and I have been working for a Presidential Commission, investigating possible violations of U.S. law by the CIA in Haiti over the past few decades. The other victims were all Haitians who were potential informants or witnesses."

Stamp grunted. "This Dickens was Haitian?"

"No. He's American, born in the South. He spent most of his life in prison. I don't know how long he's been out. He was a member of the Fortune Society, so you can check with them for details. I suspect they'll want to make the funeral arrangements; if they don't, Garth and I will."

"So what's the connection between this guy and the Haiti thing?"

"There isn't any."

"That makes the two of you the connection between the six other vics and this one."

"I guess."

"I take it he was a client of yours?"

"Yes."

"What was his problem?"

"Nothing important—and nothing to explain this. Lou Skalin down at the Fortune Society referred him to us. I told you he was a poet, and he took his work very seriously. Somebody was plagiarizing his poetry—altering it slightly and submitting it to poetry journals under another name." I paused, glanced at Garth. He was staring at me impassively, watching and waiting to hear what I was going to say. "I told him we'd look into it sometime in the future, when we weren't so busy with this other thing."

The detective thought about it, shook his head. "A man comes to you because somebody is plagiarizing his poetry, and he ends up being killed in the same manner as six other victims who were all Haitian and linked to an entirely different investigation. That doesn't make any sense, Mongo."

"That's right," I said, again glancing at Garth. My brother was still staring at me, and he had raised his eyebrows ever so slightly. "It doesn't make any sense."

"That's it?"

"That's it, Henry. Sorry we can't be of more help."


*Back in my office I stared down* into my coffee cup, seeing Moby Dickens' face on the surface of the steaming black liquid. Rage had supplanted sorrow, and the strong coffee did nothing to wash away the taste of bile in my mouth.

"You kind of caught me by surprise back there, Brother," Garth said quietly from where he was sitting on the couch. "Why didn't you tell Henry the whole story? Kranes is the connection."

"Sure he is," I said to the black face floating in my coffee. "I want another crack at Kranes myself, and I don't want to have to stand in line."

"Mongo, have you thought this through?"

"Ah. A metaphysical query if ever I've heard one. You mean, do I appreciate the irony in the fact that I gave up Moby Dickens to a right-wing prick, and thus somehow marked Moby for death, but won't give up said right-wing prick to the police, who would then immediately move to apprehend the people responsible, all the way up the ladder?"

"You've thought it through."

"Now here's a poser for you. How many police, FBI agents, reporters, public relations spokesmen, and baying politicians does it take to change a lightbulb?"

"So many that we'd never see the light. I get it, Mongo. This time I'm going with you."

"For sure," I said, looking up at him and nodding. "I'll need your take on whether or not he's giving me straight answers. As far as the police and FBI are concerned, they're going to find Moby's poems and Jefferson Kelly's imitations anyway, if and when they search his apartment, and they can do with them what they want." I paused and took a deep breath, but my rage still burned. I abruptly swept the computer printouts and other papers off the top of my desk with my forearm. "Fuck this report. I'll give them a report. I swear I'm going to find out who killed him, Garth."

"And why he was killed."

"Yes."

"You think Kranes could be directly involved?"

"Anything's possible, but I can't see it."

"Maybe he whispered to his CIA buddies something to the effect, 'You've got a problem, and I've got a problem, and will nobody rid me of this potential embarrassment?'"

"So the CIA says, 'Yes, sir, we'll send out our voodoo hit squad right away, and dump the body in the Fredericksons' backyard so they'll know you're not a man to mess with. Teach 'em a good lesson.' That's more stupid than even they're capable of—and Kranes himself may be a lot of things, but stupid isn't one of them. Kranes sits on the Intelligence Committee, so he pretty much knows what we're up to. He'd know about the voodoo ritual killings. He doesn't want to be embarrassed by having the fact that he's a plagiarist made public. So his solution to the problem is to arrange for an unbelievably brutal murder where we could immediately link him to the victim? I don't think so. In less than a dozen words to Henry, or to the press, I could have made sure that William P. Kranes did nothing else for the rest of his life but answer questions about plagiarism and murder."

"Whatever the reason, it *was* unbelievably stupid, if for no other reason than they've made you seriously angry."

"You've got that right."

"But we're agreed it was our same voodoo boys who did the killing, not some copycat who may have read about the others?"

"And who picked Moby as a random victim?"

Garth nodded. "Just making sure we look at all the possibilities."

"That surgery is bloody, but distinct. It was our boys."

"Agreed."

"*Why?*" I said, pounding my fist on the desk. "Even in the unlikely event that the CIA would do any kind of wet work to protect Kranes's little secret, why not just put a bullet in Moby's head and dump him off some pier? Why whack him in a way that immediately focuses our attention on them and Kranes?"

"Good question. And yet we're agreed that the company is responsible, in the sense that they run these killers, and somebody ordered them out."

"It is most seriously bewildering."

Garth smiled thinly as he gestured toward the papers strewn over the floor at the side of my desk. "Maybe their intent was to distract us from our pressing work at hand."

"If that's the case, they've certainly succeeded."

"Could we be looking through the wrong end of the telescope? Maybe they *intended* to embarrass Kranes by linking him to a murder investigation and exposing his secret."

"Kranes is not only the best friend the company has, but the most powerful. Why would they try to gut him in what promises to be their greatest hour of need?"

"Just moving the ball around the court, Mongo."

"There's no shot there."

"Which brings us to your visitor this morning. From the way you described the conversation, Taylor Mackintosh is at the top of the stupid chart."

"Deranged is a more accurate description."

"A perfect match. Deranged is also a very accurate description for Moby Dickens' murder, and the manner in which it was done."

"It would be a perfect match if not for the fact that Moby was already dead, and probably had been for hours, when Mackintosh came in here. He was ready to cut me a check for two hundred thousand dollars, which I could presumably have toted right down to the bank. He may be deranged, but he's not crazy enough to throw away two hundred thou and draw attention to himself if he knew Moby was dead, or even if he suspected that somebody planned to kill him. Besides, here's the bottom line: if you were the CIA, would you use a jerk like Mackintosh for anything?"

"Come on, Mongo. They use people like Mackintosh all the time. You know that."

"Yeah, you're right. But in this case, what would they have been using him for? To deliver a message to us about a black ex-convict and poet who's about to be offed by their own voodoo hit squad?"

Garth grunted, nodded his head. "It's not only seriously bewildering, but surpassingly strange."

"Well," I said, putting aside my coffee mug and pressing a button on my intercom, "it's time to begin getting unbewildered. We don't have a money trail to follow, so we'll set off down the stupids trail."

"Yes, sir?"

"Francisco, get Margaret in here or hire a temp. You're about to become coauthor of our report to the Presidential Commission. It means you'll have to bring yourself up to speed on everything we've done to date, finish organizing it, and compose a first draft—which, incidentally, is probably going to be the final draft. You can use my office and files, but I'm afraid I've made a bit of a mess back here."

"I have copies of everything on diskettes, sir, and I believe I am up to speed."

"Bless you."

"Thank you for the opportunity, sir."

"Before you do anything else, call Mel over at the William Morris Agency. They may represent Taylor Mackintosh. If they don't, ask Mel who does. Then get a message to his agent that I want Mackintosh in my office at the earliest possible opportunity for an early Thanksgiving, and if he's not here within twenty-four hours it's his old turkey ass that's going to get basted."

"Sir?"

"Just make sure Mackintosh gets the message. He'll understand. Then call William Kranes's PR people. Tell them you're a reporter for some newspaper and see if you can't find out his schedule for the next few days. I want to know where to find him on short notice."

"Yes, sir."


*I spent the rest of the afternoon re-*sorting papers and preparing a detailed outline for Francisco to follow. I was on my way out of the office when the phone rang.

"Hello?"

"Mongo, it's Lucas Tremayne. I've been trying to get hold of Garth. He's not up in his apartment, and his answering machine isn't on."

"Are you home?"

"Yes."

"If you look out your window in a little while, you'll probably see him cutting the grass. He's up in Spring Valley paying a courtesy call on Carl Beauvil, bringing him up to date on some of the things that have been happening around here. He's got some chores to do around the house, so he's staying there overnight. Or you can leave a message with me."

"I'll go over to see him later, but I want you to know this too. I'm sorry it took so long for me to take care of this business, but it's not a subject Haitians—even those who know and trust me—like to talk about, even among themselves."

"Uh, what business and subject are we talking about, Lucas? As I recall our last conversation—"

"You'll recall I said I wanted to help. I memorized the photograph you showed me of the voodoo altar, and I had one of my storyboard artists do a rendering from my description. Then I started showing it around the Haitian community up here."

I sighed. "Not a good idea, Lucas. Not a good idea at all."

"I finally got some answers, Mongo. I found a voodoo priest who'd talk to me. I know what the symbols mean, and why the altar was set up that way."

"So do we, Lucas. I talked to Fournier. He said the Spring Valley victim was using his picture as an icon, praying to him like he would to a saint. He was asking forgiveness for his sins, or something like that."

There was a silence on the other end of the line that lasted for several seconds. Finally Lucas Tremayne said, "I don't know why Guy

Fournier told you that, Mongo, but it's bullshit. I have absolute confidence in my source, and he tells me that the arrangement of the symbols and objects on that altar is what he calls a 'protection array.'"

"The general was praying to Fournier for protection?"

"No, Mongo. The victim was praying for protection from Fournier. I don't know what Fournier did to that man, or what the man thought Fournier was going to do to him, but the victim was absolutely terrified of him."

# CHAPTER 8

*G*uy Fournier wasn't listed in the telephone directory, so it was back to Faul Hall. I'd set my alarm for 2:00 A.M. I rose, dressed, packed an appropriate computer diskette and some simple burglary tools in a duffel bag, then headed out and took the subway downtown. I got off near the university campus and spent a half hour casually strolling the perimeter, checking out security. There were a couple of guards on foot and two in a marked car, but all in all the security didn't look any tighter than it had been when I'd taught there years before. Finally I darted across the campus, keeping to the moon shadows under trees and beside buildings, until I reached Faul Hall. I used the weighted end of a rope to snare the bottom rung of the fire escape on the side of the building, then clambered up to the third floor and the window of Fournier's office. Using a penlight, shielding the glow with my body, I carefully checked around the edges of the frame for thin wires or a magnet that would indicate an alarm system that would have to be disabled. There wasn't any. The window was locked, but it took me less than half a minute to jimmy it open with a small crowbar. I climbed in over the windowsill, then closed the window behind me so as not to attract the attention of any passing security guard. Then I went directly to the computer console.

Unlike the rest of the office, the workstation was uncluttered, without even a sheet of paper or a manual on the steel table that supported the IBM computer. Using my penlight, I searched through the three drawers in the table, but found no diskettes—not even blank ones. Whatever information there was might be on the computer's hard drive. I turned on the machine and executed a few keystrokes to see what kinds of programs and menus I was dealing with. On one list I found indications of several coded files, markers on the trail to what I was looking for. I inserted the blank diskette I had brought with me, then executed a command to copy Fournier's files. That would take a while. While the computer whirred away at its busywork, I went over and sat down behind Fournier's desk.

Again using my penlight, I searched through the desk drawers more carefully, found nothing but a collection of paper clips, rubber bands, and a dozen sharpened pencils of various colors that he apparently used to grade student papers. There were no filing cabinets. Except for whatever might be in his computer, Dr. Guy Fournier traveled light in the record-keeping department.

The books and magazines on his desk, many of them marked in a dozen or more places, all looked like standard armament for a professor of comparative religion. I leaned back in the chair, played the thin pencil of light around the office, over the stacks of literature piled on the floor to the hundreds of books filling the bookcases. I wondered how he found anything when he was looking for it.

Or how anybody else would find anything, assuming they were looking for something that could not be reduced to bytes of data and stored in a password-coded computer file. The place still looked more like a storage area than an office, but it also looked like an excellent place to hide something; burying it in plain sight, as it were.

I got up, began working my way slowly through the stalagmites of literature on the floor. There were books and magazines in French and English on everything from anthropology to Zen Buddhism, and they were all covered with a film of dust that made it evident they had not been consulted in some time. The books in the bookcases appeared the same, all covering appropriate subjects in the professor's field of expertise, and all coated with dust. Or almost all. When I got to a section of shelves that were almost directly across the room from the desk, at a height that would be just about at Fournier's eye level, there were a number of books that looked as if they had recently been referenced, at least to the extent that they had not had time to collect a film of dust since their last outing. I selected one, a thick tome on Zoroastrianism, stretched up, and pulled it out. When I held it upside down by the edges of its binding and shook it, three photographs fell out and floated down to the floor.

Well, now.

I sat down on a pile of French professional journals and shined my penlight over the photos. All three were eight-by-tens, black-and-white, and appeared to have been taken with a telephoto lens. The shots were obviously of three different groups of pro-life activists demonstrating outside abortion clinics. The faces of the shouting men and women were appropriately twisted with emotion, their gestures eloquent, the messages on the placards they carried evocative. The clinics were not identified, but seemed to be in different parts of the country; there was the trunk of a palm tree visible behind a demonstrator in one photo, and another photo showed a group standing atop a snow bank. But the pictures had something else in common besides the fact that all three were of activists demonstrating outside abortion clinics. The same two men—young, white, the expressions on what otherwise would have been fresh, midwestern faces twisted with hate—appeared in all three of the photographs. Although it was unclear whether or not they knew each other, in all three shots the heads of the two men had been circled in red. I looked on the backs of the photos, but there was nothing there, nor on the front, to identify them. I stared at the faces for some time, trying to etch them into memory, then replaced them at random in the book—hoping Fournier wouldn't notice they weren't where they had been—and put the volume back on the shelf.

The next book I took down seemed out of place in Fournier's large—if rarely used—professional library. It was a compendium of recent Supreme Court decisions with the complete texts of opinions rendered. As I leafed through the volume I could see that a number of sections had been marked with yellow highlighter; all of the marked sections were from the bitterly dissenting opinions of two justices, Mabel Roscowicz and Richard Weiner, both now deceased. Taped onto the back cover was another photograph, a formal group portrait of the Supreme Court justices in their robes. The heads of Richard Weiner and Mabel Roscowicz had been circled in red ink.

The thrill of discovery was thoroughly dampened by a sudden chill and the wave of nausea that rippled through my stomach. I was staring at the text and photograph, wondering whether I should risk searching around through other offices for a copying machine, when the lights suddenly came on.

I dropped the book and spun around, clawing for the Beretta in my shoulder holster, then froze when I saw Guy Fournier—unshaven, dressed in rumpled khakis, loafers with no socks, and a thin leather jacket over a pajama top—standing in the doorway, a Glock with some kind of custom-made silencer held steady with both hands and aimed directly at my chest. The thick, white hair crowning his triangular head was uncombed, but there was nothing sleepy about his piercing eyes. I'd completely missed his security apparatus; it wasn't some bell or siren rigged to the door or window, but must have been an alarm in his quarters that went off when his computer was turned on. A big tut-tut on me; but I needed those computer files, and by lingering I did find the marked photos of the pro-life activists and the two dead justices. In any case, that decision was now obviously moot.

"What kind of voodoo shit is this?" I asked in a mild tone, nodding toward the gun in his hand. "Isn't that cheating?"

"This is nine-millimeter voodoo shit," Fournier replied evenly in his resonant bass. "It's used for dealing with people who walk around as well armed as you do these days. Toss your gun away."

"Where?"

"Anywhere you like, as long as it's well beyond your reach. Use your thumb and index finger to remove it from the holster."

I did as I was told, lifting the Beretta from my holster and tossing it to my right, in the general direction of his desk. The gun skipped across the tops of two stacks of magazines, then clattered to the floor.

He continued, "Now the other one."

"What other one?"

"The Seecamp you carry in an ankle holster on your right leg. Again, use only your thumb and index finger to remove it."

"Jesus," I said, bending over and pulling up my right pant leg, "you've been reading my mail. The company must have quite a dossier on me."

"You and your brother. Do it, Frederickson. Then step away from the stacks to where I can see your whole body. Don't try to bandy words with me or attempt any other kind of distraction. I'm an excellent marksman, and if I even sense that you're going to try to move on me, I'll put a bullet through your heart."

"Wouldn't that mess up your tidy little office here?"

"I'll just throw out your corpse along with the bloody books and magazines. The office needs cleaning anyway."

"Yeah, but how much fun would that be? I thought you specialized in heart removal."

"You're trying to bandy words, Frederickson. I have warned you."

I regarded the black bore of his Glock, which was steady and remained aimed directly at my chest. I took out the Seecamp, tossed it after the Beretta.

"Now sit on the stack of magazines to your right. Both feet flat on the floor, hands on your knees."

I sat.

"How did you find out about me?"

"Didn't you read in my dossier that I'm arguably the world's premier private investigator?"

"I thought we had solved the problem of people being willing to talk to you and your brother."

"Now there's a startling admission if ever I've heard one."

"It doesn't make any difference. You'll eventually tell me who steered you toward me, and that person will pay with agony and death."

"Wooaa. Tough talk for a company lackey. You can certainly kill me, but what you can't do is impress me. It doesn't take any balls to inform on your people, torture, and kill when you do what you do. Now, if you really *had* been what so many Haitians believed you to be, that would be a different matter. The immigrants and exiles here consider you a hero, but all you really are is one more chickenshit informer who's been on the CIA payroll for years."

Shadows moved in his ebony eyes. He leaned against the doorjamb, blinked slowly as he regarded me. I stared back. Finally he said, "Informer? Hardly. It appears you don't know as much about me as I thought you did. I fear you don't appreciate my . . . work."

"So you're a full-fledged field operative, maybe a case officer. Big deal."

He grunted. "We don't have titles in my department. My department doesn't have a name. We don't keep organizational charts."

"You work for Ops."

He raised his white eyebrows slightly. "Do I?"

He most certainly did. But the idea of a kind of Shadow Ops within Ops, working off the chart, in a manner of speaking, and perhaps unbeknownst to even the director of Operations and the roster of case officers was not totally out of the question. They grew some pretty strange weeds at Langley. If my situation had not been so dour, I might have found the notion intriguing, as opposed to irrelevant to my present circumstances. I said, "Being a high-profile Catholic priest in Haiti must have cramped your style."

"Not at all. My non-Church duties were purely administrative."

"What did you administrate?"

"Haiti. You could consider me the chairman of the board of the controlling entity. People like Papa and Baby Doc and the generals were essentially my CEOs, and the Ton-tons and Fraph their administrative assistants. The business really ran very smoothly for decades. Then, of course, things got out of hand. But we'll be back there, the same as we'll be back in Cuba after Castro dies."

"With the Mafia providing your CEOs and administrative assistants."

"Exactly. Now you're beginning to understand."

"What do you call this department of yours among yourselves?"

"We don't call it anything. You're a fool, Frederickson, just like this president. What the hell good do you think this silly report of yours is going to do? You can't touch us. They could fire everybody at Langley—every clerk, secretary, director, analyst, and field operative—and blow up the building, and it wouldn't matter to us. We can't be rooted out, only transplanted. We're not listed on any budget; we pay our own way. The CIA is our host body of choice, but there are others."

"Interesting that you should compare yourself to a parasite."

"Ugly, but curiously accurate. Ever try to kill a tapeworm, Frederickson?"

"Hey, I'm giving it my best shot."

"It was an exercise in futility, even before you ended up here as my guest. We're the people you're really after, and, until now, you didn't even know we existed. We're invulnerable. Only a handful of people buried deep within the agency make up our organization, and none of these individuals has ever been a political appointee or a director, not even a director of Operations. So you can reorganize the CIA any way you like, and it won't affect us. Put the CIA out of business, and we'll just pack up shop and move elsewhere. After all, we only have a dozen other intelligence agencies to choose from."

"I should bite my tongue for saying this, Professor, but it sounds to me like you're whistling in a graveyard. I think you're full of shit. If you weren't worried about the report, you wouldn't have been sending out your boys of summer to butcher potential witnesses and informants."

He shrugged. "Moving is inconvenient. We prefer that things remain as they are. Incidentally, I enjoyed your remark about whistling in a graveyard. Your dossier describes you as occasionally witty, and I'm glad I've had this opportunity to appreciate your wit firsthand."

"Why the *hell* did you kill Thomas Dickens, Fournier? That didn't even make the halfwit mark. It made no sense at all."

"You killed him, Frederickson. You killed him the moment you decided to try to use him to further the cause of people of your political persuasion."

"I wasn't planning to use him for anything at all."

"That's not the way I heard it. I received information that at some opportune time in the future you were going to use Mr. Dickens to try to severely embarrass a friend of ours. The act of plagiarism itself was, of course, very trivial, but the lapse in ethics could have been used not only to tarnish Mr. Kranes's personal reputation, but also to damage his credibility and thus his political career. That would not be trivial. He's very important to our plans, and we weren't going to sit around and wait for you to drop that shoe."

"Your fucking information was wrong, Fournier!" I snapped. "That plagiarism business was strictly between Dickens and Kranes. I was just acting as a go-between. It was business, and the deal was done. Dickens never even asked the real name of the man who'd been stealing his poems, and I didn't tell him. You killed that man for nothing!"

"It seems I was misinformed," Fournier replied in a flat, uninterested tone. "Pity."

"And why *that* way?! For Christ's sake, couldn't you have just shot him?!"

I wasn't sure the lean, white-haired killer was going to answer, but he obviously enjoyed hearing himself talk, and after a few moments of reflection, he said, "I will grant you that the method of execution was perhaps inappropriate, Frederickson."

*"Inappropriate?!"*

"It doesn't make any difference now, but it could have complicated matters. One has to use the tools at hand, and some tools are blunter and less flexible than others. You can't carve scrimshaw with a chainsaw."

"What the fuck does that mean?!"

He smiled thinly, but there was no humor reflected in the black pools of his eyes. "Be patient," he said softly. "I promise you an answer."

Guy Fournier was making me very angry, and I couldn't afford to deal in any emotional currency, particularly not the very debilitating coin of anger. I took a deep breath, slowly let it out, then yawned. "Look, Professor, this has all been very interesting and informative, but I'm getting sleepy. I think I'll head home now."

"I think not. I have a surprise for you."

"I hate surprises. I don't mean to sound impatient, Fournier, but if you're not going to let me go home, tell me what the hell we're waiting for. What happens next?"

"We are waiting for my associates to be brought to me. They don't live as close by, and their modes of travel are somewhat restricted. The sequence of events after that will depend on your attitude."

"Right now I have a very bad attitude."

"I know. That can be changed."

"Now that would *really* surprise me."

"You will be taken to my place of power."

"'Place of power'? What the hell is that?"

He cocked his head, and once again the corners of his mouth curled up ever so slightly. His eyes seemed to gleam a little brighter. "You might call it my personal house of worship."

"It sounds kinky. I'll bet it isn't Saint Patrick's Cathedral. Don't tell me you actually believe your own voodoo bullshit."

"'Believe' isn't the operative word, Frederickson. Voodoo isn't really a belief system, like Judaism or Christianity. It's not a religion at all—not for adepts. The fact that it is considered as such by so many people is precisely what makes it work for true practitioners."

"True practitioners like yourself."

"Yes."

"So the fact that it's a belief system for hundreds of thousands of people means that it's not really a belief system for voodoo hotshots like you at the center of the web. Your students must have to take a lot of notes."

"There isn't time for a complete lecture."

"If voodoo isn't really a religion, what is it? I mean for true practitioners like yourself."

"A means of gathering and exercising power, of course."

"Then it's no different from any other religion—for its professional practitioners."

"Well, yes. But the voodoo priest is not so much interested in making religious career choices in order to make a living as in focusing concentration and will."

"You mean scaring the shit out of other people in order to get them to do what you want them to do."

"Exactly. Voodoo does have that in common with organized religions. The difference is the lack of attending hypocrisy. The voodoo priest makes no claim to saving souls."

"Far be it from me to defend organized religions, Fournier, but they don't serve up horror as the main course."

"Your naïveté surprises me, Frederickson. Your dossier would have led me to believe that you would appreciate the horror of the Mass, where men, women, and children delight in eating the flesh and drinking the blood of a crucified Christ."

"Of course I appreciate the horror of the Mass, but in the end it's just folks drinking wine and eating biscuits while they gawk at a statue of a man nailed to a cross. It's not the real McCoy."

"I am a voodoo master, Frederickson. You should feel honored to be . . . attended by me."

"Well, voodoo still sounds like a religion to me, and it makes my heart flutter to think that you—"

I abruptly stopped speaking, my words clogging in my throat, when my heart really did begin to flutter. A man in a gray suit, gray turtleneck, and dirty sneakers had suddenly appeared next to Fournier in the doorway, and his appearance was startling. He was over six feet, but slightly stooped, as if there was something wrong with his spine. He was either bald or his head had been shaved, and his eyes were lifeless, vacantly staring into some abyss in front of him. He was black, undoubtedly Haitian, but his flesh was ashen, virtually matching the color of his suit. He was slack-jawed, and spittle ran out of both corners of his mouth. He moved forward and was followed into the room by two other men. They were slightly shorter, but were dressed in identical gray suits and turtlenecks, and sneakers. All were hairless, ashen-skinned, vacant-eyed, slack-jawed, and drooling. The three of them looked like nothing so much as extras in some old Boris Karloff movie. Fournier said something to them in a language I recognized as Creole. Then the three shuffled forward, slowly wending their way around the piles of books and magazines, spreading out until they formed a semicircle in front of me. They stopped when they were about six feet away.

The voodoo master's chainsaw had arrived.

"My associates," Fournier said quietly.

Terror is the most debilitating emotion of all, and the sight of the three drooling, soulless men standing in front of me and staring into eternity thoroughly incapacitated me. My chest was constricted so tightly that I was having trouble catching a breath, and my back felt as if someone had pressed a slab of ice against it. If my hands had not been wrapped tightly around my knees, I knew they would be trembling. What had slouched into the room was apparently what Fournier had in mind for me, destroying my mind and will instead of carving out my heart, maybe to have me pad off and get his newspaper and slippers each morning. I preferred death the old-fashioned way, even if I had to earn it, but mostly I preferred me the way I was. My only chance of staying that way lay first in relaxing, as improbable as that goal seemed under the circumstances. Fournier apparently knew what I was thinking, sensed I wasn't too thrilled with developments, for he was now standing erect in the doorway, aiming his gun with both hands at my right kneecap. My first, panic-stricken reaction was to leap to my feet and start whaling away at the men in the gray suits, but that plan was contraindicated; I wouldn't be whaling, or standing, very long after a bullet had shattered my kneecap. A more practical plan of attack—or escape—was needed. Such a scheme was not immediately springing to mind, but maybe, just maybe, there might come a moment when a window of opportunity for survival might open for a single split second. If such a window did open, and if I was to be able to take advantage, I would need all my strength, reflexes, and quickness at peak operating efficiency, and at the moment I felt about as limber as a boulder.

It took all of my will to force myself to breathe regularly and relax my muscles. Fiercely wrestling the terror back into a crawlspace in my mind where I could ignore it for a few moments, I slowly crossed my arms over my chest, crossed my right leg over my left, threw back my head and laughed. Somewhat to my surprise, the sound really did resemble a laugh instead of a shriek. I let it trail off into a low chuckle, then shook my head and said, "Well, I'll be a monkey's uncle. There really is something to this zombie business after all."

Fournier, who had moved a few feet into the room so as to get a better aim at my knee with his gun, looked uncertain. He blinked a few times as he stared into my face, then grunted softly. "You've been described as having great courage, Frederickson. I see that the reports are accurate. I salute you."

Imagining I was just an actor in an ancient movie with my four ghoulish costars, I read the next line in my improvised script in a steely voice. "Stick your reports and your salute up your ass, Professor. Hey, when you gotta go, you gotta go, and it looks like I'm outta here. I know when it's over, and I sure as hell don't intend to give you any more satisfaction than you already have. Besides, I think this is kind of a hoot. I assume you know I've been shot, frozen, electrocuted, beaten, stabbed, tortured to the point of death, what have you. Run-of-the-mill stuff. Hey, but being turned into a zombie, or having my heart cut out in a voodoo ceremony? Now *that's* one hell of a way to end a career. Of course, when my brother finds out about it—and he will, I assure you—he won't be as amused. He'll show you some brand-new voodoo tricks of his own."

Fournier's response was to speak to the men again in Creole. The man with the matching face and suit directly in front of me reached into a pocket and withdrew a small glass vial with a cork stopper. The vial was half filled with a fluffy, yellowish powder flecked with dark green spots that could have been tiny seeds.

"This won't hurt you, Frederickson," the white-haired man said as his helper removed the cork from the vial and started shuffling toward me. I could hear the barely suppressed excitement in his voice. "This is just a little something to make you more . . . compliant. It will be much easier if you cooperate. Just breathe it in deeply, as if you were taking snuff or cocaine."

Compliant, indeed. I suspected that the main ingredient in the "little something" he wanted me to snuffle was what was reported to be tetradioxin, dried poison from the glands of the puffer fish, and all it would do to me was destroy my mind and put one hell of a dent in my nervous system. I laughed again, then threw back my head, stretched out my arms, and made loud snorting noises. "All *right!* Go for it! This should be one hell of a trip."

The moment, a millisecond, arrived. As the man with the vial leaned over to put it under my nose, he came into the line of fire between Fournier and me. I snapped my crossed right leg up, burying the toe of my sneaker into the gray-faced man's groin. Zombies apparently retained a certain amount of sensitivity in their testicles, because this one let out a most un-zombielike yowl, grabbed at his crotch with his free hand, and began to sag to the floor. I grabbed the open vial from his other hand and hurled it across the room at the startled professor. He had been about to fire at me, but his eyes went wide at the sight of the vial spewing powder and streaking toward his head, and he quickly ducked away, covering his mouth and nose with his free hand.

Since Fournier was obviously so concerned about not breathing in any of the powder that hung in the air like tinted dust motes, I took it to mean I should be likewise concerned. I sucked in a deep breath and held it. However, I wasn't going to be able to stay in a breath-holding mode for very long at all, considering how my heart was racing, and I had major distractions. The man I had kicked was still out of commission, but from somewhere inside their suits his two colleagues had produced blades that were as big as Bowie knives and curved like scimitars. I ducked as one slashed at my head, and came up and jabbed the stiffened fingers of my right hand into his solar plexus. Two down. I dodged the knife thrust of the third man and, still holding my breath but feeling as if my lungs were about to burst, leapfrogged over a stack of books and headed for the window. I paused just long enough to duck down behind the computer station, eject the diskette I had inserted, and put it between my teeth. Then I dove through the glass, covering my face with both forearms. I didn't hear the cough of the silenced gun behind me, but I did hear the bullets whack into the window frame and glass flying around me, smashing the shards of the pane into even smaller bits.

Circus time. The momentum of my dive carried me clear over the fire escape, but as I sailed through the air I reached out at the last moment as I twisted around and caught the top of the steel railing with my right hand, my breath exploding through my nose and from between my clenched teeth. I swung back and banged hard into the fire escape, which I immediately let go of when Fournier, holding a handkerchief over his nose and mouth, suddenly appeared at the window above me and pointed his Glock at my head. I plummeted as bullets ricocheted off steel and whined over my head, but managed to break my fall by grabbing the railing at the second-floor landing, and then at the first. I landed hard on the ground, absorbing the shock by collapsing my legs and rolling over twice. I came up running. Grabbing the diskette from between my teeth and gasping hoarsely for breath, I sprinted across the campus in the direction of Washington Square Park.

By the time I found a pay phone that worked I could hear the distant wail of sirens approaching from three directions. I knew where the fire engines were heading—Faul Hall, where the office of Dr. Guy Fournier was undoubtedly ablaze, destroying all his papers, books, and magazines, along with the photographs and any other little treasures that might be hidden there. I called 911 to report on four maniacs, three in gray suits who looked like zombies and the other wearing a pajama top, who were somewhere on the streets of the Village, and I urgently requested that they be picked up and held for questioning. I didn't think it was going to do much good, for Fournier and his zombies were probably already long gone in the van or station wagon that had brought the three members of the voodoo death squad to the campus, but I figured it was worth a try. When I hung up the receiver, I noticed that the pitted black plastic was covered with blood.

I stepped out of the phone booth into the faint, grayish light of the breaking dawn and looked down at my hands and front. I was bleeding from a dozen places, mostly my hands and arms, where the flying shards of glass had nicked me, but there were no bullet holes, and all of the cuts looked to be superficial, if messy. What concerned me more than the cuts was the residue of yellow powder that clung to my clothes and skin like sticky bee pollen. Under the circumstances, I decided that it was just as well I was bleeding, for I didn't want any of the "zombie dust," as I was beginning to think of it, to get into the cuts, and I certainly hoped I hadn't breathed in any of it. I needed a good vacuuming, and I really didn't care to find out how much of the stuff it took, either inhaled or absorbed through an open wound, to turn me into something gray-faced, shuffling, and drooling.

I removed two tiny slivers of glass from my forearm as I considered my next move. I needed to get washed off and patched up. Then what I wanted to do more than anything else was to get after Fournier and his colleagues, without interference or anybody looking over my shoulder. However, I knew I no longer had the luxury of independent action. A very deadly game with enormous consequences was indeed afoot, and I had no idea when the opponents were going to push their pawns out over the board—in two months, a week, a day, ten minutes. Now that they knew I was privy to their strategy, they might radically advance their time schedule. I was going to have to confer with the powers that be, and I was going to have to do it immediately—even before going home. I figured I had used up a good decade's worth of luck in the past hour or so, and I might not have any left. If I even indulged in the simple luxury of going home to get cleaned up, I ran the risk of getting hit by a truck, or squashed by a falling piano, or tripping over a curb and breaking my neck. That wouldn't be good for me, and it could be disastrous for the country.

I wanted to unload what I had found out as quickly as possible, but I wanted to do it in friendly territory, where I wouldn't be asked a lot of unnecessary questions or hassled with the observation that I was guilty of breaking and entering and burglary, if copying encrypted data from Fournier's computer was considered theft. I wanted to keep things simple, and I wanted to be on my way as soon as possible. I decided that the best place to go for my debriefing was Midtown North, where most of the cops knew me, and where the precinct commander and I had forged some pretty strong bonds as a result of a rather unusual adventure we'd shared the fall before. I went back into the phone booth to call the FBI, identifying myself and informing them that they should have an agent meet me at the Midtown North precinct station house in a half hour or so. Then I called the office and left a message on Francisco's machine telling him where I would be. I took off my light jacket and draped it over my arms. Still, I knew I wouldn't be picked up by any taxi driver, so I hopped on the subway and headed uptown, ignoring the half dozen or so early straphangers who gaped at the bleeding dwarf with an empty shoulder holster in their midst.

*t the precinct station house a paramedic patched me up while we waited for the FBI to arrive. Somebody found me a clean uniform shirt belonging to some female officer to wear, and I discarded my torn, bloody, and dust-covered T-shirt and jacket in a plastic garbage bag. In the meantime, an APB was issued to pick up one Dr. Guy Fournier and three gray-suited associates who, I assured the dispatcher, would be instantly recognizable. Fournier and his trio of drug-lobotomized killers had almost certainly gone to ground by now, but the APB was part of the drill— and it assured that cops would be on the lookout for **Fournier** if he surfaced and tried to go to his home or apartment, wherever it might be. Finally three FBI agents, all of whom I had come to know, showed up, along with the chief, Captain Felix MacWhorter, who had been called at home and who had insisted on coming in to hear firsthand what the "crazy neighborhood dwarf" was up to lately.

I told my story—most of it—and then told it again. I didn't mention the computer diskette I was carrying inside my jeans; I thought the excuse that I might be a tad forgetful, considering what I had been through, would be acceptable. If I gave up the diskette to the FBI, it was unlikely I would ever see it again, and I wanted the first run on whatever might be on it. They were going to be pissed, even

more resentful than they already were of Garth and me and the Presidential Commission, and what they considered continued and un-
warranted intrusion on their turf, but I couldn't have cared less. I also
neglected to mention my source for the information about the voodoo
altar and Fournier's picture, or Fournier's affectionate mention of
William P. Kranes, or the link between Kranes and the mutilated
corpse in Central Park that had been Moby Dickens. I assumed both
the NYPD and FBI could already have discovered the link themselves, if they'd worked hard enough at it, and I still wanted first
crack at the Speaker of the House myself, before he'd been worked—
or glossed—over by anybody else. I figured I had earned that pre-
rogative.

. Garth walked in around 8:45, just as, for the third time, I was getting to the part about the zombie dust. I started all over again, for my
brother's benefit, and when I was finished I was told I could go. The
FBI agents might have suspected I was holding more than a few
things back, because they did not look at all happy; but they hadn't
been happy with me for a long time. The Fredericksons and the FBI
had history. The FBI was a crack outfit that did their job surpassingly
well, when they felt like it and when it didn't conflict with their various agendas, and they weren't a bunch of criminals, but my affection for J. Edgar Hoover's clones was only slightly greater than my
affection for the CIA, and considering some of the things they had
done to us—or failed to do for us—at critical junctures in the past, I
thought they should be grateful I told them anything at all.

"Jesus H. Christ," Garth said, looking at me and shaking his head
in disbelief as we walked out of the station house into the morning of
what promised to be a very hot and humid day and headed toward the
brownstone. "You've got shit for brains."

"Hmmm. Reading between the lines of that characteristically
metaphysical and enigmatic statement, I take it to mean you're not

pleased about something. Bad drive into the city this morning?"

"You were a fool to pull that stunt last night by yourself, Mongo," Garth said, deadly serious. "I suppose you've come that close to dying a few times before, but right now I can't think of any instances. Fournier would have kept for twenty-four hours, and longer. Then I'd have been with you as backup."

"Okay, so I got impatient. I didn't expect the evening to be that eventful. I was just going to do a little simple breaking and entering to get at his computer and have a look-around."

"There hasn't been anything simple about a single thing we've done in the past six months."

"Hey, Garth, does it sound to you like I'm arguing the point? You're right."

"Don't do anything like that again."

"I managed to make a copy of what was on his computer. Right now the diskette is threatening my manhood."

"Bully for you."

"Ah, you know how I thrive on praise. Incidentally, don't brush up against me. I've still got this yellow shit on my jeans, and I don't recommend coming into contact with it. These pants and sneakers go into a plastic bag when we get home. I'm going to send them over to Frank's lab to have the powder analyzed."

"So, you really think those guys were zombies?"

"A rose is a rose is a rose. What's in a name? I don't care what you call them. I know what I saw, and that was three men who looked worse than dead, moved like Frankenstein, and unquestioningly did whatever Fournier told them. Something made them like that, and from the way Fournier was so eager to get some of that yellow stuff into me, I'd say it's the chemical agent. I have no desire to find out firsthand what it does."

Garth put one of his big hands on my shoulder, gently squeezed it.

"After what you did last night, a little behavior modification in you might be an improvement."

"Damn, there's another one of your knee-slappers. I've always marveled at your keen sense of humor."

"You must be exhausted. We'll get you home and into a shower, and then into bed."

"We'll get me home and into a shower, and then I'll nap on the plane."

"We're going to Washington, I presume?"

"Or Huntsville. Wherever Francisco tells me Kranes is holed up for the day. We've got to stay ahead of the curve on this thing, and I've got a bad feeling that events are going to move very quickly now that Fournier has been blown. It's going to be a sprint, and we've got to haul ass if we expect to be winners at the finish line."

"Right."

When we walked into the brownstone we found a temp working Francisco's station and Francisco at the computer workstation in my office. He looked up and grimaced, obviously startled by my police uniform shirt and somewhat battered appearance. "Sir, what happened to you?! Your—"

"Not now, Francisco," I said, holding up my bandaged right hand. "I got voodooed, and I'll tell you all about it another time. Right now we're in a big hurry, and I've got a couple of things for you to do."

"Of course, sir."

"Where's Kranes today?"

"Washington. At five-thirty he's scheduled to fly to—"

"Good," I said curtly, taking the diskette out of my jeans and handing it to him. "Make a copy of this and send it by messenger to Special Agent Mackey at the FBI field office. Enclose a note saying it's from Guy Fournier's computer, and I forgot I had it with me."

"Will do, sir."

"Then call the Slurper. Tell him we need him in here right away, and he should bring his toothbrush, favorite pillow, and teddy bear. He can sleep on the sofa. We'll give him premium pay. There's at least one encrypted file on that diskette, and probably more. I want to know what's in them. The files may be in French, so you might want to have a translator on call. Think speed. You sit close to him with a pad and pencil and take down everything he says, as he says it. I know he mumbles, so if you don't understand something he says, make him repeat it. The Slurper lives in the moment, and he couldn't come up with an intelligible written report after the fact if his life depended on it. His feet are only on the ground when he's in cyberspace."

Francisco ran a frail hand over his slicked-back hair, touched his pencil mustache, then made a face. "I don't think the Slurper uses a toothbrush, sir. Does it have to be him? We have a half dozen other hackers—"

"None as good as the Slurper."

"But he's *flatulent*, sir."

"There's nobody better at crashing into systems and breaking codes, and that's what's required here. Francisco, I know his personal habits are disgusting, but we need him."

"I understand, sir," he said, and slowly nodded. He had the resigned look of a condemned man about to step before a firing squad.

"Good. Now, before you do either of those two things, call Kranes's office. It's vital that you break through to talk to him personally. Mentioning my name should do the trick, but don't take any shit from secretaries or flunkies. Refuse to get off the line until someone does contact him and mentions my name. Only if all else fails do you leave a message. The message is that Garth and I are catching the next shuttle to Washington. We have to talk to him about two matters— one of important personal concern to him, and the other concerning vital national security. He'd damn well better be prepared to meet with us as soon as we get there, or we immediately call a press conference. Got all that?"

"I've got it, sir," he said, reaching for the telephone.

I started to walk out of the office, then stopped in the doorway and turned back. When you'd spent the night being shot and slashed at, sprinkled with zombie dust, and dropping from tall buildings in a single bound, it's amazing the small things that come to mind—my mind, at least. "Francisco?"

He stopped dialing, hung up the telephone, and looked inquiringly at me. "Is there something else that needs to be done, sir?"

"No. I'm just curious as to why you keep calling me 'sir.' I told you a long time ago that you should call me Mongo."

He flushed slightly. "I can't help it, sir. It's habit. You're my boss."

"Garth's your boss too. You don't call him 'sir.'"

"It's different with Garth. You're the one who interviewed and hired me."

"You don't have any prejudice against dwarfs, do you, Francisco?"

He snapped back in his chair, obviously alarmed. "Oh *no*, sir!"

"Only kidding. I seem to recall one occasion when you did call me Mongo."

He swallowed hard, said, "That was when we thought Garth was dead. I'd just given you the news. I felt so terrible for you. I'd . . . never seen you look like that before."

I thought about it, nodded. "All right, Francisco. I don't want to make you uncomfortable. I just wanted to remind you that you don't have to keep calling me 'sir' all the time."

"Yes, sir," Francisco replied, smiling wryly as he once again picked up the telephone receiver and started dialing. "Thank you."

I went up to my apartment, where Garth was waiting for me. He'd already removed my spare guns from my safe and laid them out on the bed. He'd also made me a sandwich, which I much appreciated. I ate quickly, washing down the sandwich with a glass of milk, then bagged the jeans and sneakers that had been contaminated with the yellow powder, showered, and quickly dressed in clean clothes. We were on our way out when the intercom on the wall buzzed. I went back, pressed the button.

"What is it, Francisco?"

"I was able to speak with Representative Kranes, sir. He'll see you as soon as you get to Washington. He's sending a car and driver to pick you up at the airport."

"Thank you, Francisco. Good work."

# CHAPTER 10

*T*he office of the Speaker of the House of Representatives was furnished in rococo and as large as a handball court. We were ushered into his office, and as soon as the heavy wood door closed behind us he leaped up from behind his desk. His jowly face was florid, and his pudgy hands trembled. "What's this threat of holding a press conference?!" he shouted at me as Garth and I walked across a quarter acre or so of thick, beige carpeting toward his desk. "I suppose you're looking for more money now! I thought we had a—"

"Shut up," Garth said curtly, without waiting to be introduced. "Who else besides my brother did you talk to about your problem with copying other people's poems?"

Kranes opened and closed his mouth, then slowly sank back down in his cushioned leather chair. He seemed nonplussed, totally taken back by Garth's effrontery, or his question, or both.

"This is my brother, Garth," I said as I walked up to the desk and leaned on it. "Now that the introductions are over, be kind enough to answer his question. Who did you talk to about Thomas Dickens after I visited you in Huntsville?"

"What the hell happened to you?"

"Never mind what happened to me. We may get to that. Answer the question."

Still appearing thoroughly confused, Kranes looked back and forth between Garth and me with narrowed eyes. Finally he said, "I didn't talk to anybody about him. You think I'm a fool?"

"That's what we're here to find out."

"As you surmised, it wasn't exactly a story I wanted to get around."

"Close associates? Family? Your wife?"

He shook his head nervously. "I didn't want anybody to know— not associates, and *especially* not my family. Have you—"

"What about Taylor Mackintosh, the actor? He claims to be a real good buddy of yours. Maybe you had a couple of drinks together, wanted to bare your soul? Did you discuss this problem with him?"

"You do think I'm a fool," he said, making a dismissive gesture with his hands. "Mackintosh would be the last person on earth I'd bare my soul to. I've been avoiding him for years, and I won't even take his phone calls. The man is mentally ill."

"Think real hard. Who did you mention Thomas Dickens' name to?"

"I don't have to think hard," he replied tersely, impatience now evident in his tone. "I told you I did not discuss this matter with anyone. Now, if you're not here to squeeze me for more money, why don't you tell me why you are here? I really do have a very busy schedule."

I glanced at Garth, who looked at me and nodded once. It meant my brother the empath and human lie-detector believed Kranes was telling the truth. Garth took a gold-plated Montblanc pen out of a holder on the desk, wrote on a piece of the Speaker's embossed stationery, and shoved the paper under the other man's nose.

Kranes glanced down at the message on the paper, then looked up sharply. "What?!"

He abruptly stopped speaking when I put a finger to my lips, then motioned with my head toward the door to his office. He hesitated a few moments, then abruptly rose and walked with us to the door, which Garth held open for him.

"Get rid of your Secret Service detail," I said quietly.

"I can't get rid of them."

"Then tell them to keep their distance. I don't want anyone else hearing what I have to tell you—yet."

Kranes spoke to his receptionist, then said something to the two dark-suited men sitting nearby. There was no discernible response from either of them, but when we walked through the warren of outer offices they stayed behind at a respectful distance. When we reached the wide marble hall outside the suite of offices, Kranes immediately turned on Garth and snapped, "What the hell do you mean, my office is bugged?!"

"It means just that," Garth replied evenly. "If what you've told us is the truth, then your office must be bugged."

I said, "Let's go get a drink, Mr. Speaker. I think you're going to need one."

"I don't want a drink!" he said sharply, wheeling on me. "I have important appointments all day, and I have to catch a flight to California at five-thirty! I demand you tell me why you think my office is bugged, and who you think is bugging it!"

Garth abruptly gripped the other man by the elbow and gently but firmly escorted him the length of the hallway and around a corner. Kranes walked very stiffly. I followed, and behind me I could hear the click of the Secret Service agents' heels on the marble as they followed behind us all. I wondered what they were thinking about this little *tête-à-tête* between two strangers—if we were strangers to them—and the man they were assigned to guard.

When we had all made it around the corner, Garth stopped, turned the Speaker toward him, said in the same soft, even tone, "The CIA is bugging your office, Kranes. They've probably got your home wired too. They take the old adage about keeping friends close and enemies even closer very literally. They're keeping tabs on you and your visitors because you're very important to them and all the other fascists in this country."

"That's ridiculous, Frederickson! And don't you imply that I'm a—"

"Keep your voice down. They intend to make you president."

That got his attention. He looked inquiringly at me, then back at Garth. "Are you serious?"

"If you think this is a joke, that was the punch line. You are the CIA's candidate for president, and they know how to run a hell of a winning campaign. Ask the Chileans."

Something, perhaps an image of himself sitting in the Oval Office, must have flashed across his mind, because he suddenly paled, and his breathing became rapid and shallow. "But I don't understand. It isn't my time yet to be president. My advisors all tell me—"

"The company doesn't give a shit what your advisors say," I interrupted, "any more than they care about what you want or the electorate wants. They're apolitical. They only care about what they want, and they want you in the White House. Right now there are some very strange things going on outside these hallowed halls, and what they all add up to is that the CIA is trying to engineer the assassinations of the president and vice president. *Voilà.* President William P. Kranes."

Kranes's eyes went wide, and he glanced nervously at the two dark-suited men standing perhaps fifteen yards away, at the head of the corridor. "The two of you are crazy," he said in a sibilant whisper. "'Assassination' isn't a word one tosses around lightly up here."

"Oh, that toss was too light for you? I guess I'll have to try my curve, slider, and fastball. You obviously haven't been paying attention to what Garth and I have been telling you."

"Leave me alone," he said, actually shying away. "If you think there's a plot to assassinate the president, it's the Secret Service you should be talking to, not me."

"I've already told the FBI, and I have to assume they've briefed the Secret Service. I can assure you that the FBI is taking this very seriously; check with them yourself if you think Garth and I are telling you some fairy tale. All that can be done is being done, you can be sure. There's nothing the Secret Service can do at the moment but take their usual defensive posture. That's one reason—but not the only reason—we're here talking to you."

"Why me?"

"Because you're in the best position to stop it."

"What on earth—"

"You and I had a deal," I said, stepping closer to him. "It turns out you didn't break it, and neither have I—so far. Our deal is the reason I haven't mentioned the plagiarism matter to any of the authorities, and I've been talking to a hell of a lot of them. But your connection to Thomas Dickens is going to surface eventually. There could be a lot of history written on what's happened, and what's about to happen. Some people may even charge Garth and me with culpability in the assassinations of a president and vice president because we withheld certain details explicitly linking you to Thomas Dickens and CIA-run killers. It's going to come out, Kranes, especially if the president and vice president end up dead—because then *we'll* have to disclose it. It's better that you do it, now, if you want the history books to be kind to you. Then you'll work with the Secret Service. Like I said, you're the person in the best position to put a stop to their plan, or at least slow it down."

Kranes eyed me suspiciously. "How could the poetry incident possibly have anything to do with this supposed assassination plot you're telling me about, and what would discussing the incident accomplish except possibly destroying my career? Maybe that's what this is really about. You said you talked to the FBI, but why aren't the two of *you* working with the Secret Service?"

"Because we don't have anything else to contribute—except you—and we have bigger fish to fry."

The jowly man shook his head and laughed nervously. "This is absolutely preposterous! You *are* trying to destroy my career! Either that, or you're both insane. You say there's a plot to assassinate the president and vice president, but you don't have time to work with the Secret Service because you have bigger fish to fry. What fish would those be?"

"Finding the murderers of a certain poet, you fat shithead," Garth said, his tone soft as a knife slicing through silk as he abruptly reached out and grabbed Kranes's tie close to the knot, lifting the startled and suddenly choking Speaker of the House up on his toes. "You think that's funny? You make me sick. Every time I hear one of you loudmouthed bigots talk about the need for a 'color-blind society,' I want to puke. Where was your mouth back in the sixties? Your family probably owned slaves."

"Uh, Garth," I said, touching my brother's arm as both Secret Service agents started running toward us, reaching inside their suit jackets. "Perhaps it might be a good idea to leave the extraneous political discourse for another time."

The men were almost on us when Kranes, still up on his toes and red-faced, raised his right hand and desperately signaled for the agents to stop. They stopped, but their hands remained inside their suit jackets, on their guns. Finally Garth released his grip on the man's tie. The two agents backed away, but not as far as they had been.

Kranes, wide-eyed, turned toward me. "What's he talking about? What poet?"

"Thomas Dickens is dead, Mr. Kranes," I replied. "He was savagely murdered in the same manner as possible witnesses in our Haitian investigation were murdered, which is one reason we know for a fact that the CIA was behind it. The only reason they could have had for doing it was to save you possible embarrassment before or after your swearing-in. They don't want any distractions or questions about your character. Now, if I didn't say anything to anybody, and you didn't say anything to anybody, and Thomas Dickens didn't even know your real name, it led us to deduce that the CIA must have your offices here and in Huntsville bugged. Get it?"

"My God," Kranes whispered hoarsely. He was beginning to look frightened. "But why . . . how . . . ?"

"You're third in the line of succession, Mr. Speaker. Remember?"

"But I don't *want* to be president," he replied absently. "At least not yet."

"Irrelevant. With the president and vice president dead, you're it. There's no election to wait out."

Kranes shook his head stubbornly. "But the next election is only a few months away . . ."

"I think they may have plans for the next election, and we'll get to that. In the meantime, three months is enough time for you to go through a whole laundry list of executive actions, appointments, and proposed pieces of legislation that would sail right through the Congress that your party controls. The first one or two hundred things you'd want to do as president are totally predictable; they're only interested in two of them."

"This is insane. You're slandering—"

"The men who founded OSS, and later the CIA, were idealists as well as cowboys. They were our great white knights, our Paladins, during the Cold War. A lot of good men and women sacrificed their lives to protect this country's secrets and steal the enemies'. Members of the Operations Directorate rode into hell to save Western civilization."

"Are you being sarcastic, Frederickson?"

"I am not. It's the simple truth. But it's also the truth that when they rode out again they had begun to look to some of us just like the KGB. By the end of the Cold War, they'd only gotten uglier. The Russian KGB is, at the most, operating at very low voltage in their Federal Security Service over there. Ours is still sparking away, and these people are very dangerous."

"I don't agree at all with that characterization of the CIA," Kranes said stiffly.

"I understand that, Mr. Speaker. I also understand that, even if you did agree with it, you'd argue that it's necessary to have such an organization working clandestinely, even occasionally beyond the law, because we still live in a dangerous world, and we have to be prepared to fight fire with fire. Even if our guys have turned ugly, the enemies they're up against are even uglier. You'd say we have no choice but to trust our own people."

"That is exactly right."

"You consider the aims of the Presidential Commission Garth and I are working for to be potentially very damaging to the national security of the United States. In fact, given that the potential damage should be obvious even to a child, you believe the members of the commission and the people working for them to be not only unpatriotic, but very likely traitorous."

"That is also exactly right," he replied, drawing himself up slightly and thrusting out his chin. "You state my feelings more precisely than I ever would, Frederickson."

"So what would one of your first acts in office as president be regarding this commission?"

"I'd disband it," Kranes answered without hesitation.

"Bingo. And what about the work the commission has already done up to this point? What about all the files and raw data? What if the final report had almost been completed?"

This time he did hesitate, and I prompted him with a wiggling finger. "Making public any part of the commission's raw data and speculations would be damaging to national security," he said at last. "I'd order it sealed."

"Right again. You're on a roll. Those are the two things the CIA desperately wants, the only two things they give a damn about. Do you see now why they're so eager to get you into office as quickly as possible? If they can get you into the Oval Office now, even for a few weeks, it won't matter to them who wins the next election. The issue will be moot; the commission will have been disbanded, and all its work product safely squirreled away, or even shredded."

He hesitated again, but this time I didn't prompt him. I wanted him to think about it, let the picture I had painted come into sharper focus and unfold before his eyes. Apparently he didn't like what he was seeing, for he finally said, "I have many personal friends in the CIA, Frederickson. They're decent people. Patriots. They'd never be part of a conspiracy like the one you're describing."

"And they're probably not. Don't misunderstand me, Kranes; I'm not suggesting that the director of the Central Intelligence Agency sits down every morning for a breakfast meeting with the heads of his departments to discuss how this operation is going. The director doesn't know about this, I can assure you; probably only an infinitesimal number of people over at Langley even have a *hint* of what's going on, and the director of Operations himself probably isn't one of them. This gig is being run by a handful of people in Ops, but the work of this handful of unelected people could be enough to subvert the Constitution of the United States and change the very nature of this country for the foreseeable future. The fact that such a tiny number of men *could* effectively operate within the confines of such a massive organization shows the extent of the corruption of the entire organization itself. They're supposed to *stop* people like this, not nurture them, but the CIA isn't going to be able to stop them any more than they were able to bring themselves to finally stop Aldrich Ames, after it was too late."

"This is all just sheer speculation," Kranes said tightly, but fear had once again appeared in his eyes.

"This is a classic operation, Kranes. Ops is manipulating clowns and madmen to bring about a desired end. It's the kind of thing Ops does best, and when they're at the top of their game—which they seem to have been in this case until they murdered Thomas Dickens and gave us a peek under the canvas—there's no covert organization in the world better at it. What they've done in this instance is to whisper in the ears of an assortment of lunatics. They've spun dreams of what life in the United States would be like under the presidency of William P. Kranes, what a hard-right president could accomplish with the aid of a hard-right Congress. Prayer in schools three times a day, and maybe even the United States officially declared a Christian country, all gun control laws rescinded, *Roe versus Wade* overturned and all abortions outlawed. The list of right-wing social goals is endless, and there'd be no problem in achieving most, if not all, of them once you were in office. After all, you'd immediately have two vacancies on the Supreme Court to fill. You'd waste no time in naming your choices, have the immediate support of Congress for whoever you nominated, and we all know what type of judges you'd offer up. That's the package the CIA has been offering."

Kranes's flesh had turned the color of a dirty dishcloth, and his breathing had become shallow and slightly hoarse. "You can't be implying that—"

"Wake-up call, shithead," Garth said in the same soft, silky tone.

I nodded. "Our conspirators, for whom the CIA as an organization bears responsibility, offed two Supreme Court justices, guaranteed."

"But one died in a car accident, and the other in her sleep!"

"Keep your voice down. They were murdered as part of a pact between these Ops renegades and their flunkies who are going to do their big kills for them. There are any number of wacko Right-to-Lifers who believe that killing abortion *doctors* is their ticket to heaven. They don't care if they die themselves, because they consider themselves blessed. Imagine how fast they'd get their rocks off at the notion of just two kills that would lead to the total banning of abortion throughout the country. Well, the CIA—our renegades, if you will—has at least two of these people on tap, and they're the boys who are going to carry out the assassinations. With the right equipment and training, you can kill anybody, provided you don't care about dying yourself. These folks can't wait to die carrying out this mission; they believe they're going to wake up in heaven on the lap of God."

Kranes licked his lips, then swallowed hard. He looked at Garth, then back at me. "I can't believe any of this is possible. Where's your proof?"

"You can believe Thomas Dickens is dead. Call your people in New York and check it out. He was blinded, and had his tongue, heart, and testicles cut out of him."

Kranes blanched, put a hand to his chest, shook his head. "If these CIA conspirators of yours were so clever as to murder two Supreme Court justices and make their deaths look like accidents, why wouldn't they have done the same thing to Dickens—especially if their purpose was to shield me? After he was killed in . . . that manner . . . the two of you came running right to my office. Why do something that results in the opposite of what was intended?"

"A good question," I conceded reluctantly, disturbed by the tiny gleam of triumph in his eyes, "and we'll have to get back to you on that. My best guess is that there was some initial confusion at operation headquarters on how best to handle the situation. Conflicting signals may have been sent out, and those signals got crossed. There may have been an abrupt change in plans. Their first mistake was in automatically assuming that I wasn't on the level during our conversation in your Huntsville office, and that I intended sooner or later to use the plagiarism incident to publicly embarrass you, no matter what I said. Working on that assumption, they first decided maybe they should just try to buy me off, which is how Taylor Mackintosh wound up in my office waving a checkbook. But before the bagman even got there, somebody may have successfully argued that my purpose was ideological, and it was unlikely I could be bought off. So then a decision was made to change course and simply remove the core source of the problem, and then things began to go haywire. The wrong personnel were chosen for the job, just as Taylor Mackintosh had been absolutely the wrong person to send to me. I won't know how and why those mistakes were made until we can penetrate their command structure, which is that big fish we're trying to fry. But these are the things that can go wrong when you have said clowns and madmen fronting for you."

"What you're saying is that you don't have proof of *any* of this."

"Taylor Mackintosh's visit is proof that your offices are bugged. You're certainly aware of Thomas Dickens' link to you, and the manner of his death, by the same voodoo hit squad that's been killing our Haitian witnesses, links that killing to the CIA—and our conversation in your Huntsville office. I could go on, but how much proof do you need?"

"Dickens' murder could have been a copycat killing."

"Don't go into denial on me, Kranes. I've seen incriminating photographs that link an admitted CIA operative both to the dead Supreme Court justices and the two Right-to-Lifers the CIA will use as shooters. Unfortunately, that evidence was destroyed in a fire. The FBI can't be more than one or two hills behind us on this, but by the time they gather enough evidence to convince you of what's going on, it could be too late. As of this moment, Garth and I are the only people who are aware of your link to the latest murder victim."

*"Presumed* link to—"

"By the time the FBI gets around to talking to you, you could already be in the Oval Office—and the chair is going to be covered with your predecessor's blood. Events are going to be moving very quickly now. The other party's convention starts in less than a week; that will present one opportunity for the assassins. But the attempts could come sooner, or later; today or tomorrow—or in two weeks, a month. Just so long as you have enough time to do what they know you'll do, which is to wipe out this commission and its findings. That's why we're here talking to the object of their affection. It really doesn't make any difference whether or not the FBI finds the connection between you and Thomas Dickens; whether they do or they don't, you're still the only person who can put a stop to this thing now."

"You can't expect me to—"

"Your invisible handlers are a government unto themselves, Mr. Kranes. They rule a country where there are no maps or boundaries to begin with, but where they're constantly trying to project and expand their power. Their loyalty isn't to the United States, it's only to themselves. You dream of some pastel, mythical country called the United States as you imagine it was forty or fifty years ago, a place that never really existed, and you pander to the prejudices of millions of people who share the same fantasy. The people who are trying to manipulate *you* dream of a falling eagle, a kind of fascist America where they're free to do just about any damn thing they please without fear of any embarrassing questions being asked by bothersome elected officials who suspect some of the pranks they pull may not really be in the best interests of national or global security. It's a game to them, Kranes, a Great Game, and the only thing they're interested in is being able to continue playing it without interference. The game is an end in itself. Over the course of the past six months, because they now perceive a very serious threat to their power, they've murdered six Haitians, one American poet, and two Supreme Court justices. Now they're poised to murder the president and vice president—all so that you'll be president long enough to guarantee their survival, and maybe beyond that. They may have promised their flunkies an all-out effort in the November election to keep you in office, and then maybe a repeal of the Twenty-sixth Amendment. All this just to wreck the commission and quash its report. They don't give a damn about the wreckage they'll leave behind."

Kranes shook his head stubbornly. Although it was not warm in the air-conditioned building, tiny beads of sweat had appeared on his upper lip. "Just for the sake of argument, let's say everything you're telling me is true."

"It is. Believe it."

"And you think I can stop it all simply by going to the FBI and Secret Service and telling them Thomas Dickens was killed because I was caught copying some of his poems?"

"No. You stop it by resigning."

"What . . . ?"

"You heard him, shithead," Garth said. "If you really want to do something for your country, get the hell out of office. The CIA wants you at the altar because you're every fascist's sweetheart. Break up the engagement, and maybe they won't burn down the church."

We'd really hit him where he lived. Kranes wiped at the sweat on his upper lip, but it didn't do any good; even larger droplets had appeared on his forehead, and were rolling down over his pudgy cheeks. He didn't react at all to my diplomat brother's words. We had painted him a nightmare scenario, but that didn't seem to upset him as much as the word "resign."

"You don't have to resign from Congress, Mr. Kranes," I said quietly. "You can go right on representing the people of Huntsville, Alabama, and you can keep on saying whatever you want to say. But you have to resign from your Speaker's post. And you should call a press conference and do it this afternoon, right after we leave. You have to take yourself out of the line of succession. Announce that you're backing a moderate—any moderate, if there's one left in your party—to replace you in the post. Then the CIA will abort. The consequences of failure are too great for them to risk carrying out the assassinations with no guarantee they'll be able to cover their tracks and control whoever winds up being president. Without you as a quick and easy solution to their problems, these people will back off their plan, hunker down, and leave it to the rest of the agency to concentrate on trying to find a way to defend themselves against the charges in the commission's report. Your party, and your ideas, won't suffer; someone to your liking will almost certainly win the November election. And you may even get to keep your little secret."

Kranes did not reply. He took a handkerchief from his pocket and wiped his face, then stared down at his shoes.

It was Garth who broke the silence. "He's not going to do it, Mongo," my brother said evenly. "Fuck him. Let's stop wasting our time and get out of here."

"Is my brother right, Mr. Kranes?" I asked, stepping closer so that I could look up into his face. "Are you going to give these murderers what they want?"

His reaction was to quickly step around me and away from both of us, shuffling a few steps further down the corridor. When he looked up, his face was flushed, his eyes wide. "There's too much at stake for me to resign from the Speaker's post."

Garth said, "Oy."

I said, "What?"

"We're on the verge of making this country right again, and I'm the man who brought us here. My party needs my continued leadership. You come to me with this completely wild story, without any solid proof of any of it, and you expect me to immediately step down from my position of leadership. Even if you're not consciously part of any scheme to bring me down, the two of you may still be pawns of people who are trying to do just that. All of this could be part of some elaborate liberal plot to derail me and our plans for this country. At the very least, I have to have time to think about it. I will not—"

Somewhat to my surprise, he abruptly stopped speaking when I raised my hand. I said quietly, "While you're mulling it over, here's something you can do on your own to check into this wild speculation and the possibility of some liberal plot against you. Loosen up with some of your buddies in the Twilight Zone who you've been avoiding lately for fear they'll embarrass you. Take, say, Taylor Mackintosh out for a few drinks. He may wind up telling you a few things you don't want to hear."

Garth raised his right hand and cocked his thumb and index finger like a gun, which he aimed at the man standing down the hallway. Then he smiled thinly, winked, and said, "You've been warned. Don't come crying to us if you end up having to be president."

# CHAPTER 11

W e arrived back in New York at 4:45, were at the brownstone by 5:30. There was a long, black limousine with smoked windows parked at the curb. A bored-looking chauffeur in a uniform that was too tight for him leaned on the hood, smoking a cigarette. The occupant of the limousine, wearing a tan summer suit, two-tone brown cowboy boots, and his muskrat top was waiting for us in Francisco's office.

"It's about time you got here!" Taylor Mackintosh snapped, leaping off the chair he'd been sitting in as we entered. "My agent said there was a message that you wanted to see me right away! I'm not used to waiting on people, especially people I figure are looking to get some money from me!"

"Mr. Mackintosh," I said sweetly, "you can't imagine how happy I am to see you. Hang on just a couple of seconds and I'll be right with you."

As Garth leaned on the reception desk, I went to the back of the office and peered through the venetian blinds at the scene in my office, which was already littered with pizza cartons, sandwich wrappers, and empty soda bottles. The air in there, I knew, would be foul. The source of all this putrescence, the best hacker in New York City or any place else, as far as I knew, was a three-hundred-pound, red-haired man in his mid-twenties who was sitting at my computer console smacking his lips and mumbling to himself as his stubby fingers fluttered over my keyboard. The ripped T-shirt he wore was thoroughly sweat-soaked and covered with food stains. Francisco, looking thoroughly dejected but resolute, sat next to the man, pad and ballpoint pen in his hands, dutifully recording the Slurper's mumblings. I tapped on the window. The Slurper just kept working away, but when Francisco looked up and saw me he beamed as if I was the Second Coming. He motioned toward the closed door of the office, as if asking permission to escape for a few moments to talk to me, but I smiled and shook my head. His smile vanished. I motioned for him to come over and close the blinds, then turned away from his plaintive, pitiful gaze as he did so.

"Now, Mr. Mackintosh," I continued in the same sweet tone as I turned to face the indignant-looking actor. "I don't believe you've met my brother. Garth Frederickson, this is the famous Taylor Mackintosh."

Garth grunted as he reached out and rested his hand on the telephone.

"Skip the formalities, Frederickson," Mackintosh said curtly, reaching inside his suit jacket. "How much money do you want to make this poetry bullshit go away? I assume that's why you wanted to see me."

"Actually, it isn't. Did you know I used to be in the circus?"

His hand stayed inside his jacket, and he scowled. "What?"

"I wanted you to come in so that I could show you how high I can jump. Check this out." I took three quick steps, leaped into the air high enough to snatch the toupee off his head, came back down and bowed a couple of times, holding out the ratty hairpiece for his inspection. "Pretty damn impressive, huh?"

Taylor Mackintosh's face turned the color of brick, his eyes went wide, and he put both hands on top of his bald head. "What are you *doing?!*"

"Here," Garth said, picking up the telephone receiver and holding it out toward the thoroughly astonished man. "You'd better call nine-one-one."

Mackintosh, still holding his hands on top of his head, bolted for the open doorway, but when he got there he found me blocking it. He came to a halt, spun around toward Garth. "Are you *crazy?!*"

"You shouldn't believe all those rumors floating around about us," Garth replied evenly.

"Why should I call nine-one-one?!"

"Because it looks to me like Mongo is getting ready to beat the shit out of you. You'll need emergency medical services, and then you'll want to press charges. I'll call the tabloids myself. I would recommend the headline, 'Dwarf Pulverizes Gingivitis Spokesman.' Sound all right to you?"

His eyes wild, Mackintosh tried to make a dash over, around, or through me. I smacked him on the right thigh, not hard enough to risk damaging old, brittle bones, but with sufficient force to give him a charley horse and assure his attention. He sat down hard on the floor, kneading his thigh and making whimpering sounds. If I hadn't had such a vivid image of Moby Dickens' mutilated body in my mind, I would have felt thoroughly ashamed of myself.

"Nine-one-one?" Garth intoned mildly, extending the telephone receiver out even further. "If you tell the police your life is in danger, they may get here before Mongo snaps your scrawny, red neck."

"What do you *want?!*" the old man wailed.

I stepped closer to him, until my face was only inches from his, and I could smell the garlic, fear, hate, and death on his breath. "Your problem resolved itself," I said, looking hard into his pale eyes. "Thomas Dickens is dead. He was murdered."

His mouth dropped open, the blood drained from his face, and he began to frantically crab-walk backward. I followed right alongside, keeping my face in his. I could tell by the expression on his face and the panicked look in his eyes that he was receiving the news for the first time. He stammered, "I didn't . . . I didn't have anything—"

"Also, some of your like-minded friends are planning to assassinate the president and vice president. You know anything about that?"

He came up hard against the opposite wall, hit his head. He cringed and tried to turn away, but I grabbed his chin and turned his face back toward me. "Answer me!" I spat at him.

Even with my hand cupping his chin, he managed to vigorously shake his head back and forth. "They talk," he whispered hoarsely. "But it's only talk."

I released his chin, stepped back. Garth came over, and together we lifted him up off the floor and into a chair, where he slumped dejectedly. I filled a cup of water from a jug in the corner of the office, brought it to him. "I'm sorry I had to hurt you, Mr. Mackintosh. But there are some serious problems we're dealing with here, and we need information quickly. There isn't time to be polite."

"Who makes this talk?" Garth asked quietly.

"Dozens of people," Mackintosh mumbled, not looking at us. "It's no secret that a lot of people hate this administration, and Bill Kranes would be president if something happened to those two pinkos in office now. You can't blame people for wanting what's right for the country."

I leaned close to him again, forcing him to look into my eyes. "Are you part of a conspiracy to assassinate the president and vice president of the United States, Mr. Mackintosh?"

"God, no!"

"Do you know anybody who is?"

"No. I told you it's all just talk. People get mad and they vent their feelings. They just want to get the Communists out of our government once and for all."

I glanced at Garth, who nodded to indicate he believed the old man was telling the truth.

"Whoever murdered Thomas Dickens is doing a lot more than just talk, Mr. Mackintosh. Who told you to come in here the other day and offer me money?"

He hesitated, and I again gripped his chin. "Paul Piggott," he mumbled, averting his gaze.

"And who is Paul Piggott? What's his relationship to you?"

"He's vice president of Guns for God and Jesus." Mackintosh paused, rubbed his aching right thigh with both hands, then continued, "He called and told me Bill Kranes was having a problem with some nigger claiming the Speaker had been copying his poems. That could be embarrassing if the charge was made public, and Paul said it sounded like a blackmail scheme since you were fronting for the nigger. He told me I should have a talk with you, offer you money, and see if I could pay you off. A couple of days later he called to tell me I should forget the whole thing, but by then I'd already come here to see you."

"Was this your own money you were supposed to use?"

He shook his head. "Guns for God and Jesus has a checking account."

"Gingivitis doesn't have a teacup to piss in. You've probably got less than two hundred members, and you're lucky to come up with money for postage to send out some nutty mailing every few months. Suddenly you've got a hundred and fifty thousand dollars to pay off a blackmailer?"

"There was money put in the account for that purpose."

"Where does the money in this account come from?"

"I don't know," he said grumpily. "I'm not their accountant."

"Give me a check."

Now his mood brightened. He looked at me accusingly. "So you *do* want money!"

"No, I said I wanted a check. In fact, give me the whole checkbook."

He hesitated, and Garth pointed toward the telephone. Finally he withdrew a book of checks issued by a bank in Arizona. I took it from his hand, put it in my pocket, continued, "Why did Piggott pick you for this errand?"

"He never said. I'm the public relations spokesman for our organization, and I guess maybe Paul figured this was a public relations problem."

I glanced at Garth, who rolled his eyes toward the ceiling. "Jesus Christ," he said. "We're dealing with a bunch of imbeciles."

"What, is that supposed to be a news bulletin?"

Garth leaned over the chair Mackintosh was sitting in, put his mouth close to the other man's ear. "Where can we find this Paul Piggott? Give us an address and phone number."

The old man looked plaintively at his toupee, which I still held in my hand. I gave it to him, and he quickly mashed it on top of his head. It was off by about ninety degrees, but actually looked better than the way he normally wore it. "He doesn't have an address or phone number. He lives off the grid in Idaho."

"Off the grid?"

"He's in a survivalist compound, getting ready for the upcoming race war with the niggers and other mud people. They don't have electricity or telephones. When he wants to contact me, he goes into town."

"You use the word 'nigger' again, old man, and I'm going to wash out your mouth with soap. How does he get his mail?"

"A post office box in town."

I asked, "Have you ever been to this compound?"

He nodded.

Garth retrieved a pad and pencil from Francisco's desk and dropped them in Mackintosh's lap. "Draw us a map, old man. Make sure it's a good one."

# CHAPTER 12

"Well, well," Garth said. "Check out the action over in the clearing at two o'clock. Are those your poster boys?"
I trained my own pair of powerful binoculars in the direction where Garth was pointing, and nodded. "That's them."

We were squatting down just inside a copse of fir trees on the crest of a mountain top in north-central Idaho, with the horses we had ridden in on tethered in the trees behind us; they were blowing and munching contentedly on a mound of oats we had spread out over the ground. Below us, at the foot of the mountain, sprawled a kind of ramshackle shanty town of tents and lean-tos scattered about among towering cords of stacked firewood. The only structure in the compound that looked even semipermanent was a crudely built log cabin set off from the tents and lean-tos in its own clearing an eighth of a mile or so to the south, and we assumed this was the lair of the Maximum Leader. To the north, where a rutted dirt road snaked into the compound, there was a wart of shiny black metal that was a motorcycle parking lot. We'd hoped to find Guy Fournier taking some rest and relaxation at the isolated compound, despite Mackintosh's description of the group, but from the moment we'd trained our binoculars on the site we'd realized this would not be a particularly hospitable spa for a Haitian, no matter how light-skinned. This was the neo-Nazi chapter of Gingivitis, biker division, with a scurvy band of long- and short-haired, greasy-looking, leather-clad young to middle-aged wannabe storm troopers wandering about, all armed to their swastikas with everything from enormous Magnums sticking out of their waistbands to Uzis slung over their shoulders. Some of the men wore bandoliers stuffed with ammunition, most of it not of a caliber that would fit the assorted automatic weapons they carried—whether this was just stupidity, or a bizarre form of costuming, we didn't know. There were perhaps a half-dozen women, all standing around smoking cigarettes and looking bored. Nazi regalia was everywhere, from the crude swastikas painted on the tents and lean-tos to the helmets some of the men wore.

The sartorial standouts in this motley crew were the two young men off in the clearing taking target practice under the watchful eye of a man wearing a leather jacket, despite the heat, wrap-around sunglasses, and a black fedora pulled low over his forehead. The shooters were clean-shaven, wore crew cuts, were untattooed, and wearing Oxford shirts with button-down collars. They could have come to the compound straight from church choir practice, and they were the same antiabortion protesters whose heads had been circled in the photograph I had found in Guy Fournier's office.

The target practice the two young men were taking was specialized, obviously in preparation for some special occasion. There were two straight-backed chairs placed a few feet apart in which the men sat stiffly, as if at attention. A crude wooden platform was set up about twenty-five feet in front of them, and above the platform were strung a number of paper targets, two of them painted red. At a signal from their trainer, the men would, in unison, quickly reach under their chairs and retrieve two handguns fashioned from some kind of clear material that was probably a type of acrylic. Then they would rise to their feet, take precisely five steps forward, raise their guns, and fire one round each at the red targets. Then the targets would be torn down and carefully examined for placement of the bullets. The targets would be replaced, the guns returned to the mountings beneath the chairs, and they would start all over again. They could be getting ready for the upcoming convention, assuming the shooters had been seeded into a state delegation sitting in the first few rows of the recently converted convention hall at the Jacob Javits Center in New York, but the exercise could just as well be suited for any of the dozens of barnstorming or fund-raising events at which the president and vice president would be appearing within the weeks following the convention.

I watched target practice for a while, then set aside my binoculars, lay back on a bed of pine needles, closed my eyes, and listened to the munching and blowing of the horses behind me. I was bone tired, suffering a fatigue that was more than a little exacerbated by the fact that I was more than a little anxious about the constant headache I was enduring and the fact that I had awoken the past two mornings to find my pillow soaked with saliva.

It was our second day in Idaho, and I was also more than a bit concerned about things in general in the United States of America—or at least in this particular section of America. On the morning we had arrived we had rented a car at the airport, driven to this area indicated on the map Mackintosh had drawn for us, then checked into the nearest motel, which was about twenty miles to the east. From there we had set out on a series of preliminary sorties to get the lay of the land, as it were, and its populace. As far as I was concerned, the majority of the people we'd talked to could have come in on the last UFO shuttle, and they obviously regarded me in the same way, treating me not so much with curiosity, to which I was accustomed outside of New York, but with thinly veiled hostility and suspicion, as if I might have been cursed by God. Garth, on the other hand, with the rustic Nebraska air he had never lost and his natural reticence, fit right in; he could have been one of them, to all outward appearances, and the people took to him, forgiving him his odd dwarf companion. There seemed to be an inordinate number of retired L.A. cops.

This part of Idaho seemed to me a kind of Loonyland, an open-air asylum for mild-mannered crackpots. There were no black, brown, yellow, or red faces—at least none that I had glimpsed during that first day, and it was startling to hear people who looked like they could have stepped out of some Norman Rockwell painting calmly expounding viciousness, paranoia, and hatred to an extent that made even William P. Kranes sound like a moderate in comparison. In country stores and gas stations and restaurants we—or Garth—were told harrowing tales about an impending United Nations takeover, menacing black helicopters with inverted *V*s painted on their sides, and ZOG, which everyone in the countryside called the government, which they maintained was controlled by a mysterious Zionist organization masterminded by a man called Rothschild. The Holocaust was a myth perpetuated by ZOG—and even if a few thousand Jews had been killed by the Germans, the victims had deserved it. A large number of people living here against a magnificent backdrop of snow-covered mountains were patiently waiting for the End Times, Armageddon, the Rapture, and the Second Coming, events they confidently expected to transpire any day. We, meaning Garth, heard lurid tales of identification chips being implanted in people's skulls, and before long, ZOG was going to announce that every man, woman, and child would have to be tattooed on the forehead with the Mark of the Beast. These people didn't really want the government to change; what they truly lusted for was the end of the world, with rebirth in a Kingdom of God, under the benevolent dictatorship of Jesus Christ, entirely populated with people who looked and thought just like them. Through all this mad palaver over coffee, or beers, or lunch counters, Garth just kept on grunting and nodding. I kept looking away in embarrassment and anger. Certainly not every soul expressed these views, nor did everyone appear to be racist and anti-Semitic, but there were enough in the region to make me feel most uncomfortable, slightly disoriented, and almost totally alienated from the country of my birth. The insanity in the atmosphere had nothing to do with education, or birth rates, or school lunches, or the National Endowment for the Arts; these people's ignorance was willed, their superstitions and hatreds carefully cultivated and nurtured, and as far as I was concerned they deserved William P. Kranes and his dedication to make them even poorer and more ignorant, and he deserved a nation filled with them. They might represent the buttocks end of his constituency, but he shamelessly pandered to them. Thanks to people like Kranes, the sickness of these people was poisoning the country, spread through the veins and arteries and capillaries of America by rabid and irresponsible radio talk-show hosts who, for rating points and money, both fed and manipulated these people's ignorance and hatred. Perhaps in the end our efforts were senseless, and it did not make any difference whether or not the assassinations took place right on schedule, nor whether or not the CIA had its way with all of them. In the end, a democracy got the democracy it deserved, and the people had certainly spoken loud and clear in the last election. I was beginning to seriously consider the notion that, basically, America was a nation of nitwits.

I was sick of it all, and I was afraid. I just wanted to get our business wrapped up and go home, and I wanted to stop drooling in my sleep.

Throughout the day we sat, watched, and waited. The two shooters practiced for two more hours, then drove off with their trainer in a

Jeep. The merry band below whiled away the rest of the afternoon wandering around and showing off their guns to each other, the women continuing to smoke and look bored. After nightfall we sat through a cross burning during which everyone got drunk. A half hour after the last reveler had stumbled off to his or her lodging, we began clambering down the mountainside under the faint glow of a half moon. On his right hand Garth had donned a weighted black leather glove, a souvenir of his long-ago days as a county sheriff when he'd had a lot of territory to cover, with little help, and the hot prairie wind made a lot of people unpredictable and dangerous.

We came down behind Paul Piggott's cabin and went around to the front door, where Garth knocked. There was no answer, and he knocked again, harder, while I looked down the pathway behind us to make certain we were unobserved. Finally the door opened, and Paul Piggott, silhouetted against the light cast by two hurricane lamps, stood staring at us somewhat uncomprehendingly with bleary, greenish eyes that were the color of jungle mud. His long black hair hung in greasy ringlets around his puffy face. His shirt and sleeveless leather jacket were open, and his paunchy beer belly hung down over his wide leather belt.

"Howdy, Pilgrim," Garth said in his John Wayne drawl as I drove the stiffened fingers of my right hand up through rolls of fat into the man's solar plexus. "The little dogie and I are doing a survey to see what the folks in this area think of vigilante justice and fluoride in the water."

The breath exploded out of Piggott in a beery, belchy whoosh, and as he doubled over I brought my stiffened fingers up into his larynx, not hard enough to crush and kill, but with sufficient force to keep him talking in a hoarse whisper for an hour or two; it was a neat trick I'd learned from Veil Kendry, my *sensei*. Garth placed his hand on top of the man's greasy head and shoved him back into the crude, one-room cabin. I followed after Garth, closing the door behind me. Garth stood in front of the wheezing, doubled-over man in the center of the room, waiting for Piggott to catch his breath, and then, as Piggott suddenly lunged for him, swatted the man in the face with the back of his gloved hand, breaking the biker's nose, knocking out two teeth, and sending him crashing onto a sagging, ratty sofa bed set up along one wall.

Garth unhurriedly pulled up a stool and sat in front of the couch, and while he waited for our breathless and bleeding host to compose himself, I looked around. Guns of all shapes and sizes were mounted on the walls, which were also festooned with Nazi flags and other regalia that loomed eerily and almost seemed to wave in the flickering light from the hurricane lamps. Cases of beer were stacked up on either side of the doorway. In one corner were a grill and two cans of Sterno, and in another a grimy, stained, portable toilet, apparently for use when it was raining, or too cold—or when he was just too lazy—to use the latrine outside. Against the wall opposite the sofa was a table, and on it was set, most incongruously, a shiny shortwave radio powered by four chunky dry cell batteries linked in series; the outside aerial had been too thin for us to see through binoculars.

Finally I turned and went to stand beside my brother, who was leaning forward on the stool, crowding the cowering Piggott, who was dripping blood from his broken nose and mouth all over his bare chest and stomach. The man's eyes were glazed with shock, and he had the look of a cornered animal.

"So, Paulie," Garth said in a casual tone. "How's the assassination plot coming along?"

Piggott wiped his mouth with a trembling hand, then spat blood to the side, over the armrest of the sofa bed. "Who the hell are you?" he croaked, massaging his bruised larynx with his bloody right hand.

"We are the marvelous flying Frederickson brothers," I replied, rapping my knuckles on his left kneecap. "We're annoyed by something that happened to an acquaintance of ours, and we're going to take it out on you. My advice to you is to simply answer my brother's questions the first time, truthfully, because he gets impatient easily. Don't bother trying to lie, because the man's a veritable human lie detector. You're liable to lose the rest of your teeth."

He didn't take my advice. He obviously recognized the name, for he drew his breath in sharply. Then, whether out of misguided bravado or an even greater fear of someone or something else, he suffered a severe attack of stupid. "I'll die before I tell you anything," he rasped, then spat blood at my brother.

"Suit yourself," Garth replied evenly, then hit Piggott so hard on the side of the head that the man catapulted over the armrest and crashed to the floor, where he lay half conscious, moaning and holding his head as he drew his legs up into a fetal position. Garth rose from the stool, walked across the room, and took a shotgun from a mount on the wall, then came back and pressed the wooden stock against the man's temple. In the same easy tone, he continued, "If I crack your skull open, how much shit do you think I'll get on my shoes?"

"All right!" Piggott burbled. *"All right!"*

"When and where are the assassinations scheduled to take place?"

"I don't know anything about any assassinations!"

"Wrong answer," Garth said, tapping the stock none too gently on the man's head. "We saw the two shooters going through their paces this afternoon. Do you expect us to believe they were tuning up for duck season?"

"I don't know what those two plan to do," Piggott whispered in a barely audible voice. "I don't even know their names, or the name of the guy who brings them around. I was just told to let them practice here. Nobody's supposed to even talk to them."

Garth took the stock away from the man's head, then tossed him a dirty pillow from the sofa bed. Piggott pressed the pillow to his beer belly, wrapped himself around it.

"Do they ever stay in the compound?"

"No."

"Where are they now?"

"I don't know. I never know when they're going to show up to practice, and I don't know where they go when they leave."

Garth apparently believed him, for my brother's response was to look over at me and shrug his shoulders.

I asked, "Where's Guy Fournier?"

Piggott moved his head slightly so as to look at me. His eyes shone with pain, humiliation, and fear. "I don't know any Guy Fournier. It sounds like a frog name, and I don't know any frogs."

"What makes you so accommodating to these people who come here and go as they please? They're obviously not the types you normally associate with."

"I'm just following orders."

"Whose orders?"

"A woman. I don't know her name. She talks to me on that radio over there."

"Jesus Christ," Garth said. "It's like the fucking Wizard of Oz."

"Pay no attention to the woman behind the radio."

"It's the truth!" Piggott wheezed.

I walked over to the radio, turned it on, and tapped the microphone. "Maybe I'll give her a buzz. What frequency does she use?"

"The one it's locked on. It's the only frequency on the radio that works."

That was interesting. It was also interesting that the steel casing of the radio didn't have a serial number in the place where one would normally expect to find it, nor anywhere else that I could see.

It looked like a specialized piece of company equipment. I considered the notion that beneath his tattoos and greasy hair and potbelly Paul Piggott might be a highly skilled, expertly camouflaged, and very gutsy CIA operative, but just couldn't wrap my mind around the idea. He was just one more company pawn, like so many of the other people we were wading through. I asked, "Do you have a code name?"

"No."

"How do you contact this woman when you want to have a chat?"

"I don't. She contacts me when she wants to talk. I carry a beeper when I leave the cabin. When it goes off, I come to the radio and turn it on."

I leaned over the microphone, pressed the switch on the base. "Hello, hello, hello? This is spook radio. Anybody out there? Over."

I released the switch and turned up the volume, but there was nothing but the crackle of static on the speaker. When I turned the dial, even the static disappeared. I looked over at Garth. "What does your bullshit antenna tell you?"

My brother shrugged again. "It indicates he's telling the truth."

"Things just get curiouser and curiouser."

"It makes sense that they'd seal these pinheads off tighter than a bulkhead."

I walked over to Paul Piggott, who had rolled over on his back and pressed a dirty handkerchief to his broken nose in what appeared to be a successful attempt to stop the bleeding. I asked, "Does the name Thomas Dickens ring a bell with you?"

He didn't answer right away, and seemed to be thinking about it. He rolled his eyes first to the right, then to the left, and finally back to me. "I think that's the name of the nigger you were using to—"

He abruptly stopped speaking and sucked in his breath when I rested my foot on his bulging stomach. I pressed down, but not too hard. Piggott was finished, and needed only to be asked the right questions. There comes a point, probably already passed in this cabin, where a little appropriate physical persuasion becomes torture. I did not need nor want to inflict any more pain. I said, "Watch your mouth."

"For Christ's sake, is that what this is all about?!"

"What did you think it was about?"

"What do you want from me?!"

"Who told you to call Taylor Mackintosh and tell him to come to my office and try to bribe me?"

"The woman on the radio," Piggott mumbled, rolling over, getting to his feet, and collapsing once again on the sofa bed. "I'm answering all your questions. Your brother isn't going to hit me again, is he?"

"That depends," Garth said quietly.

"What exactly did this woman say to you?"

Piggott took the handkerchief away from his face, touched his crooked nose, winced. "She said you were using this nig—this African American to blackmail some guy by the name of Cranny, or Crans, or Kranes. I had it right at the time, but I'm not sure of the guy's name right now. She said this African American was going to claim that this Crans guy had stolen some poems. It didn't make a whole lot of sense to me, but the woman said it was important."

I glanced over at Garth, who looked as incredulous as I felt. I asked Piggott, "You don't know who William P. Kranes is?"

He regarded me with a combination of suspicion and fear. "That's the guy's name. I don't know who he is. Should I?"

"Do you have any idea who you're carrying out these little chores for?"

Light glinted in his murky eyes, and the corners of his bloody mouth pulled back in a malevolent grin. "People who are going to make this country a fit place for decent Christian white folks to live in again."

"That's encouraging. Precisely what did this woman want you to do?"

"She said the situation was unclear, and she wanted to explore it—those were her words. She said it looked like you and the African American guy might be cooking up some plan to make this Cranny guy look bad, and she couldn't allow that to happen. I was to send some suit from our organization to talk to you and see if you and the African American guy would take money to make the problem go away. I didn't understand how there could be so much fuss over some poems, but she insisted it had to be taken care of. The suit would be authorized to offer you up to two hundred thousand dollars to keep quiet about whatever it was you knew. A couple of days later she gets back to me and tells me to forget the whole thing, that the problem was going to be handled a different way, but by then I'd already called Mackintosh."

I removed the checkbook I'd taken from Taylor Mackintosh from my pocket, flapped it in front of Piggott. "The money would have been taken from a Guns for God and Jesus checking account?"

"Yeah."

"Where do you get that kind of money?"

"The woman and her people put money into the account when we need something, or when they want us to do something that requires cash."

"Why did you pick Taylor Mackintosh as your bagman? Is he the only suit in your organization?"

"No, but he's the most famous. He's a movie star. I figured you'd be impressed."

I glanced over at Garth, who sighed and looked down at the floor. I knew what he was thinking, shared his sadness and outrage, and sense of total frustration. In the final analysis, Moby Dickens had lost his life because of no other reasons than the company's paranoia, indecision, execrably poor choice of personnel to task, and the sheer stone stupidity of those personnel combined with Guy Fournier's hubris and indifference.

"Hey," Piggott continued. "You want to tell me now what's going on? How come you two have got such a hard-on for me?"

I looked at him, replied, "Thomas Dickens was murdered by people associated with your lady friend on the radio."

He just couldn't help himself; he leered, then barked, "Good! One less nigger we'll have to kill when the war starts."

Uh-oh. I'd obviously been wrong about Piggott being finished, and his psychotic hatred appeared to have given him a second wind. I considered smacking him in his broken mouth, but didn't have the stomach or heart. Besides, considering his remark, it was beginning to occur to me that Paul Piggott had not really found the beating he'd already taken all that unpleasant, and I didn't want to do him any favors. Garth apparently felt the same aversion—although he might well have some other punishment in mind for Paul Piggott, like a quick death. He walked across the room to where a collection of knives was mounted on the wall and selected a huge Bowie knife. Then he walked back to Piggott and pressed the tip of the blade up under the now thoroughly terrified man's chin. For a moment I was afraid he was going to drive the blade straight up through Piggott's skull, but he didn't. Instead he lazily worked the tip back and forth in the sweaty flesh until a tiny hole had been opened in Piggott's quivering jowl. A drop of blood became a stream that ran down the man's throat and over his chest.

"Garth . . . ?"

"Not to worry, Mongo," Garth replied in a whisper. "Everything's under control. I'm just lowering his blood pressure."

"Hey, all I ever did was send around somebody to try to lay a lot of money on you!" Piggott burbled. "I didn't kill the African American guy!"

I said, "We know that. Let's get back to your lady friend. What makes a big macho guy like you so eager to act as a gofer for some woman you've never met?"

Piggott's eyes were wide and crossed as he gaped down his nose toward where the tip of the Bowie knife was stuck in his jowl. "Take the knife away," he mumbled. "I can't talk."

Garth took the knife away from the man's jowl. Piggott cowered as he pressed his blood-soaked handkerchief to the fresh wound in his throat. He croaked, "Are you going to kill me?"

"A distinct possibility," I replied. "The only thing you've got going for you is my brother's deep sympathy for the mentally handicapped, and your continued cooperation. Answer my question. Why are you so hot to do everything this woman tells you? Because she and her people give your group money?"

In an instant the light in his eyes had flickered from fear to hatred, and he glared at me. "I don't have any say where that money goes," he said through clenched teeth. "And none of it goes into my pocket. I do what she asks because she and her people get things *done.*"

"Explain. Start by telling us how you got your hands on this particular radio in the first place."

"It was delivered a little more than a year ago, along with some batteries and the beeper."

"Who delivered it?"

"Some guy in a pickup truck. He didn't say anything—just put the radio and stuff down on the ground and gave me an envelope with a grand inside along with a note. The note said the radio and money were from people who wanted to help us fight ZOG. It said that if I was really serious about fighting for the rights of white Christians, I'd take the radio, set it to that frequency, and wait to be contacted. Me, I'm not stupid, so I figured it was just the goddamn government trying to trick me into doing something they could nail me for. But I figured it couldn't hurt to set up the radio and see what happened, so I did. Then the woman started calling me."

"And she asked you to do certain things?"

He shook his head, mumbled, "Not at first. I wouldn't have done anything for her in the beginning because I didn't have any reason to trust her. She said she understood that, so she was going to provide me with what she called her bony fideys. She said her people were going to do certain things to show me I could trust her, and they did."

"What did they do?"

"They killed people," he replied nonchalantly, wiping blood off his chin. "Kikes, niggers, spicks. Mud people. So-called community leaders around the country. First I'd get newspaper clippings about some troublemaker. Then, a few days later, I'd get an obituary notice saying the man or woman had been killed in an accident. I knew they were no accidents, because I'd been told about them in advance."

I shook my head, swallowed hard to try to work up some moisture in my mouth. "This still goes on?"

"Sure, it still goes on. ZOG is still in control, isn't it?"

"Who delivers the clippings?"

"A guy on a motorcycle. He doesn't stop. He just drives in, drops an envelope with the clippings on the ground, then drives off again."

"Does he have a schedule?"

"No."

"When was the last time he was here?"

Piggott thought about it, shrugged. "Last week—a couple of days after that lady kike on the Supreme Court died."

"The woman on the radio told you that Mabel Roscowicz was going to die?"

"I just said so. I knew about the guy who died just before her too. Any outfit that can take out two ZOG kike justices like that is one I'm going to take seriously. That's why I take orders from the woman."

"So what else has this woman asked you to do besides send somebody to try to bribe me and provide a shooting range for the two crew cuts?"

He looked away. "I said I didn't kill the poem guy. I didn't have anything to do with that. I wasn't even told about it."

"That wasn't the question. How many people have you and your friends here killed?"

"We haven't killed anybody. And the woman hasn't asked me to do that many things. Our main orders are to sit here and wait."

"For what?"

"To fight ZOG when the time is right. The woman says there are big changes coming in the country, and we're going to be foot soldiers on the front lines." He paused, glanced back and forth between Garth and me, then continued, "You're both white guys. You'd better start thinking about lining up on the right side before it's too late."

Garth said, "Pretty slim pickings here, Mongo. This is just a reserve unit of thugs and errand boys who probably don't know what day it is."

"Yeah, well, the trip hasn't been a total waste of time. Paulie here will make a colorful witness to the mystery lady's predictions. Also, we now know that they're not planning to use snipers at long range; the shooters plan to do their work up close and personal. The information will help the Secret Service."

"Maybe, maybe not. The president and vice president aren't going to let the Secret Service lock them up in a closet until November. The shooters get to pick the time and place, and they expect to die. It's going to be hard to stop them."

"True. But we've done our bit for the Republic. We have verification that the two justices were murdered. The FBI will want to chat Paulie up, and he shouldn't be too hard to find if and when congressional hearings are ever held."

Piggott's voice was coming back. "Hey, wait a minute!" he said, sitting up straighter. "I'm not testifying to anything! You guys are likely to be dead soon! ZOG will be on its knees!"

Garth ignored him. "Yeah, but we've used up two days going on three, and we're no closer to finding Fournier or identifying his associates in the company. Those are the people you and I are after."

I nodded as I sighed in resignation, then walked across the room to the radio with the single, preset frequency. "This is a dandy piece of CIA equipment. No serial numbers, but experts might be able to trace some of the components and identify the manufacturer, who might be able to link it to the company. Too bad it's too heavy for us to lug out of here."

"What do you mean, CIA?" Piggott said with genuine indignation. "The CIA's an arm of ZOG!"

"They're the people you've been taking money and orders from, shithead," Garth replied without looking at the man.

I walked around the radio, peered through a cooling vent on the side. I'd turned the radio off, but there was a small blue bulb still glowing inside. I felt my stomach muscles tighten. "You leave this radio on all the time, Paulie?"

"What, do I look stupid? That would run down the batteries. I turn it on when the woman wants to talk to me."

"When she contacts you on your beeper?"

"Yeah. I already told you that."

"And you carry your beeper with you all the time?"

"Sleep with it under my pillow, carry it with me to the crapper. Those are my orders. What was that shit you were saying about the CIA?"

I reached under the table and disconnected the cables linking the radio to the dry cell batteries. When I peered through the vent again, the blue light was still on. The radio had its own internal power source, and this was not good. I glanced at my watch; forty-five minutes had passed since we'd entered Paul Piggott's cabin.

"Bad news, Brother," I said tersely. "It's like Kranes's offices. The radio and beeper are bugged. Our company friends have known where we are from the moment we walked in here. They're not going to like what they've heard. I suggest we depart henceforth."

"Or sooner," Garth said, abruptly stepping close to Piggott and clipping him under the chin with the palm of his left, ungloved hand. Piggott slumped to the floor, unconscious.

Together we scurried out into the night, sprinted around to the back of the cabin, and began clawing and scrambling our way back up the mountain.

Fear is a powerful motivator, and we made it back up the mountainside in twenty minutes, not much longer than it had taken us to climb down, but the all-out exertion was wasted, and we would probably have been better off fleeing on foot in a different direction. Now it was too late.

We heard the *THWOP-THWOP-THWOP* of the helicopter rotors a few seconds before the unmarked Apache rose like some giant, malevolent bird of prey over the crest of the mountain. Mounted searchlights probed the dark mountainside, and one finally caught us in a blinding glare. We scrambled to the copse of trees, where I snatched loose the reins of our horses from a tree limb, handed Garth's to him. The horses were frightened, rearing.

Garth hesitated. "We'll be easy targets on horses, Mongo!" he shouted over the thrashing roar of the helicopter, which was hovering just above the tree line, raising a cutting, abrasive cloud of broken branches, needles, and leaves all around us.

"Not if we keep to the trees!" I shouted back, vaulting into the saddle of my horse, which immediately reared. I wheeled the animal
around and brought it under control, then reached out and grabbed
the reins of Garth's horse, which was wide-eyed with panic. "It's our
only chance! They can contact the compound by radio. There'll be a
dozen of those people after us in a few minutes, and more dozens of
searchers by dawn. I don't recall the locals as being too friendly."

Garth looked at me, then at his horse with its flaring nostrils.
"Mongo, I can't ride like you! I'm not sure I can stay on in these con-
ditions. You go! I'll keep them busy here. The helicopter can't follow
both of us!"

"Just talk to her in John Wayne and you'll be fine! Now get on the
fucking horse! Remember what I told you about posting!"

"You're on, Pilgrim!" Garth shouted as he put a foot in a stirrup,
and lunged up and onto the back of his horse.

I immediately dug my heels into my horse's side, and the animal
responded, lurching forward as I ducked under a limb, heading
through the trees. I rode a hundred yards, then sensed something was
wrong. I reined in the horse, turned to look back, and knew we were
going to have a problem.

In my years with the circus I had ridden on the backs of everything
from Bengal tigers to Asian elephants, so, even under these condi-
tions, riding a well-trained horse in a well-fitted saddle was a walk in
the park, in a manner of speaking. Not so with my brother, who wasn't
used to riding anything that didn't come with four wheels and a mo-
tor. He had barely gone ten feet. His horse, sensing the nervousness
and lack of confidence of a novice rider, was now even more panicked. He was rearing, bucking, and corkscrewing, and threatening
to throw off Garth, who had dropped the reins and had his arms
wrapped around the horse's neck, at any moment. In addition, the
backwash from the helicopter's rotors was surrounding us in a storm

of debris that was not only blinding but could also literally put out an eye. We could not go back the way we had come. When we had ridden in during the day, I had noticed dried-out stream beds leading down the other side of the mountain to a broad, forested valley, and other mountains in the distance where there appeared to be narrow canyons and washes where it would be difficult for the helicopter to maneuver. If we were going to escape, that was where we would have to go. I wheeled my horse around, rode back.

"Change of plans!" I shouted as I grabbed the reins of Garth's horse and brought the animal under control. "Just hang on to the pommel with both hands! We're going down the other side of the mountain! When we head down, let go of the pommel, grab the edges of the saddle, and lean back as far as you can! The horse will take care of the rest!"

Garth released his grip on the horse's neck and grabbed the saddle pommel. Gripping the reins of my horse with one hand and the reins of Garth's horse with the other, I urged my mount forward, out of the trees and onto the bare ground of the mountain's crest. There were perhaps three hundred and fifty yards of open ground to cover before we reached what I remembered to be a reasonably negotiable slope down the other side, and now I spurred my horse forward at a full gallop. The helicopter followed directly overhead, one searchlight turned downward and bathing us in a moving pool of bright white light. I wouldn't hear the report of a gun over the deafening roar of the helicopter rotors, but I cringed as I expected at any moment to feel a bullet ripping into my back. It didn't come, perhaps because the angle was bad, or the pilot figured he had plenty of time to run us down and give his gunner a better shot. We reached the spot I had been riding for, a rocky but negotiable dry wash that had been carved out by spring water.

I couldn't control my mount and lead Garth's at the same time, and it would have been dangerous for his horse if I tried to do so. I pulled the second horse after me over the crest and into the wash until it had reached a point of no return, then flung away the reins and shouted over my shoulder, "Here we go, Duke! Lean way back and hang on!"

I relaxed my horse's reins and leaned back, posting in the stirrups and letting my mount pick its way between and over rocks and hard-baked rills. We were over a quarter of the way down the mountainside, still with no shots being fired, when I began to think we actually might make it to the cover of a copse of trees a hundred yards further down, where we would be shielded from view and the decline was less steep. Then I sensed, rather than heard, Garth's horse stumble and go down, and my brother soared, none too elegantly, over my head and landed on his back in a clump of thorn bushes growing out of the right wall of the wash. His horse recovered, shot past me, and disappeared into the trees below.

I reined in my horse, jumped to the ground, and scrambled up the bank of the wash to the clump of thorn bushes where Garth, dazed and struggling feebly, was entangled. I drew my Beretta and fired blindly at the white light and roaring cascade of sound above my head, groping through the cloud of dust thrown up until my fingers wrapped around Garth's shirt. Still firing my gun overhead, I pulled with the other hand, trying to help Garth out of the bushes.

"Mongo, get out!"

"You get out of the fucking bushes! Come on!"

"I'm stuck! It's important that one of us get away from here! Go!"

"It's important to me that both of us get away from here! Come on, goddamn it!"

I emptied my gun and stuck it back into my shoulder holster, then worked my way deeper into the thick vegetation. I grabbed Garth's shirt front with both hands, dug my heels into the rocky soil, and tugged. Finally he broke free, and we both tumbled back down the wall of the wash to the bottom. I was reaching for my horse's reins when suddenly a net dropped down through the cloud of dust and settled over both of us. Cursing mightily, I struggled in the net. I managed to get the Seecamp out of my ankle holster, but it was a wasted effort. I felt a sharp, burning sensation in my right shoulder—not the smashing, tearing impact of a bullet, but something more along the lines of a wasp sting. I turned my head, saw a dart sticking out of my flesh near the collarbone.

"Shit," Garth said as he was struck by two darts, one in the right thigh and one in the belly.

I ripped the dart from my shoulder, and was still struggling to get out from under the net when the deafening thrashing of the rotors overhead dropped in volume and pitch to a low hum with a deep bass that throbbed in my head, chest, and stomach. The swirling dust around us suddenly became a kaleidoscope of garish greens, reds, and yellows. There was the taste of bitter chocolate in my mouth. Then, for the first time in two days, my splitting headache winked out. There was nothing to worry about. All was well with the world, so I stretched out on the ground and began to dream of emerald eagles with golden eyes and red beaks falling from a purple sky.

# CHAPTER 13

*M*y head soon began to throb again, even in my dreams, and all did not stay well with the world for long. The dreams turned to nightmares, the emerald eagles turning to black and diving for my eyes. It was difficult to fend them off, for my movements were slow and plodding, my quick reflexes gone. I had turned into a gray-faced, stumbling, drooling creature, and I felt only a dull ache in the places where the ebony raptors had torn away chunks of my flesh. Somehow I ended up in a hospital where everything was painted pink, and when Harper came to visit she screamed at the sight of me and vomited, and then ran from the room. Friends and family came to visit, but most could only stand the sight of me for a few minutes before they had to leave. Only my mother and father, ever the stoics, sat at my bedside for long hours, tears rolling down their cheeks. For my part, I just lay around in silence and drooled a lot. I desperately missed Garth, who was nowhere to be found, and never mentioned. Sometimes nurses took me out for walks on a leash. Children laughed at me and called me a zombie.

Behind or beyond the dreams was a sensation of flight, and a sound that reminded me of the steady drone of airplane engines. I would feel myself rising in the air, perhaps waking, and then I would feel a sharp sting in the arm or leg, as if someone was sticking me with a needle. Then it was back to the headache, bad dreams, and drooling.

When I did finally regain consciousness, I did not find my situation all that much improved over my nightmare dream world; some might even argue that it had deteriorated, since I was lying naked on my back on a cold marble slab of a table with my arms and legs splayed, my wrists and ankles tethered by thick leather straps attached to the sides of the table. My head wasn't restrained, so I raised it and looked around. I was not cheered by my surroundings. Garth, still unconscious but breathing regularly, lay on a similar table to my left, and he was similarly naked and strapped down. We were both spattered with blood, but it wasn't ours; apparently it had sprayed out of the bodies of the three dead Haitians, formerly Guy Fournier's little helpers, who lay on slabs to my right. Their chests had been cut open, and their hearts evidently placed in the red clay, bloodstained jars that were placed above their heads. The killings had apparently taken place within the past few minutes, for blood and gore still oozed from the gaping wounds in their chalky flesh, puddling on the brown marble and dripping to the floor.

Guy Fournier's place of power was a very large room, perhaps a loft, that had been converted into what I assumed was a voodoo temple; at least it looked pretty voodoo to me. Lighting came from red stage spots recessed in the ceiling, tinting everything the color of blood. There were dozens of *vèvès* painted on the walls and ceiling and the tile floor. I couldn't see behind me, but there were two doors, both closed, cut into the wall to my far left. On a section of wall to my right, beyond the three corpses, there hung a large set of venetian blinds, now closed.

Our host and master of ceremonies was standing in front of me with his back turned, head slightly bowed, and chanting softly in

Creole and in what I hoped was going to be a very long, solo ceremony. Guy Fournier was dressed in a long, flowing, yellow silk robe decorated with black *vèvès*. He stood before a massive altar that took up almost three-quarters of the wall space to the front. On dozens of shelves on the altar were red clay jars, carved wooden statues, *vèvès*, what appeared to be dry, withered limbs, and a collection of skulls.

I began to make a very serious effort to free myself.

I tested the bonds on my wrists and ankles, and found the straps tight. However, the strap on my right wrist seemed just a bit looser than the others. I made a fist, flexed my muscles, and rotated my wrist back and forth. There was some give to the leather. The straps were lined with sheepskin, but the blood of an unknown number of victims that had lain before me on this stone bed of death had hardened in layers that had cracked, creating a series of sharp edges. That, I thought, could work to my advantage; if I could reopen the cuts on my hands and make myself bleed before Fournier did it for me, I might be able to get a hand loose. I kept twisting my wrists back and forth, rubbing the flesh against the rough edges, staring at the back of the voodoo priest as he chatted with his bloodthirsty gods. It was a tricky business. I was drawing blood, all right, but the irritation was making my wrists swell, threatening to cancel out all my good works.

I kept at it, twisting and pulling, and then froze when Fournier abruptly wheeled around to face me. In his right hand he carried one of the scimitar-shaped knives previously wielded by his dead henchmen. The front of his robe, his hands, his triangular face and white hair were all spattered with blood. His dark eyes gleamed even brighter than usual, and he smiled broadly when he saw that I was awake. I was surprised to see that he had an erection, clearly visible as a bulge in his loose-fitting robe.

"Home delivery," I said. "I'm impressed."

"I'm so glad," he replied, his smile growing even broader. "A person in my position has certain prerogatives, and having the notorious Frederickson brothers delivered to me alive was one of them."

"I like the alive part. Look, I've got a splitting headache. You wouldn't have a couple of aspirin around here, would you?"

"I'm afraid not."

"So where are the chickens?"

His smile vanished. "You and your brother are the chickens, Frederickson."

"This your place of power?"

"Yes."

"Where are we?"

He hesitated a few moments, then quickly walked to the wall to my right, past the three corpses, and opened the black venetian blinds. I raised my head as far as I could, glanced in that direction, and found myself looking out over a familiar view, the Hudson River. New Jersey, what looked to be Hoboken or Jersey City, was across the way, which put us in a warehouse or on a pier somewhere down on the lower West Side. The sun was just setting. It looked like Garth and I were going to die close to home—in prime time, no less.

"Nice digs," I continued, then nodded toward the three mutilated bodies lying to my right. "You killed them because they botched the Dickens murder?"

"I killed them because they are no longer needed. Your investigation into Haitian matters is at an end."

"That's exactly right. I take that to mean you brought us all the way back to New York so that you could surrender to us personally."

He turned back to close the blinds, and I used the few seconds to begin twisting my right wrist again. "You do have a bizarre sense of humor, Frederickson."

"You're fried no matter what happens to us, Fournier. There are copies of all our records in a safe deposit box, to be opened and immediately delivered to the commission on the death of one or both of us. Killing us is going to get you nothing but grief from two very dangerous friends of ours. Even if your outfit does manage to assassinate the president and vice president, how long do you think Kranes is going to be able to remain in office after all this business becomes public? The FBI has to be right behind us, and then there's the NYPD, Secret Service, and even the Spring Valley Police Department working on this case. We found the connections between you, the planned assassinations, and the CIA, and so will they. This whole conspiracy is going to be blown out of the water, and making Garth and me disappear is only going to speed the process. Your best bet for survival is to agree to testify and let us take you in. The FBI will put you in a Witness Protection program. Trust me; you'll prefer that to what will happen to you when our friends track you down. And they will."

"I think not," Fournier replied evenly. "When William Kranes becomes president, the FBI investigation will go away along with the commission and its planned report. The NYPD is of no more concern to us than the Spring Valley Police Department. None of the information you and your brother have developed will ever be made public, and nobody will know of the events you've been involved in. Of course, that would not be the case if the two of you were to remain alive. Your disappearance will be treated as no more than a peculiar mystery. Your bodies will never be found. Our organization will ride out this storm, and with Kranes in power there will be no more threats. In hindsight, we should have killed the two of you at the beginning. Despite your track record, we still underestimated your persistence and investigative skills. We didn't want to unnecessarily complicate things, and we'd hoped that killing witnesses would head you off and shut you down, but it didn't. Your days were numbered long before you found me, Frederickson. But since you did find me, it shall be my pleasure to personally eliminate the two of you. It may give you some comfort to know that we consider the information you've developed and the report you were preparing to be, by far, the most potentially devastating of all the work being done by the other teams working for the commission."

"You're going to depend on Paul Piggott to keep your secrets?"

"Piggott didn't have any secrets worth sharing until you two visited him. Now he's dead."

"You move fast."

"So do you and your brother."

"So will the FBI when they finally get up to speed."

"Sometime this evening there will be a new president, and I'm absolutely confident that the FBI will be told that their investigation into the killings of the Haitians is to be given very low priority."

"The convention?"

He smiled thinly, nodded. "The president and vice president accept renomination by their party tonight, and they will appear on the platform together. It's only a matter of waiting until the nominating speeches are over. It's a pity I don't have a television set or radio here."

"Well, I hope you have a telephone, because you'd better get on the horn right now and tell your people to call it off. After our first little chat, the first thing I did was go to the police. The FBI knows all about you and the CIA, and they know about the two murdered Supreme Court justices and your Right-to-Life shooters. If those killings take place, Congress is likely to legislate the entire CIA right out of the alphabet."

"I think you exaggerate, Frederickson. The police will defer to the FBI, and it won't make any difference what the FBI knows, or what you told them. The FBI is nothing if not committed to the chain of command, and the director will do as President Kranes orders. The new president will not want to shock the country even more, and he will not want the good name of the CIA sullied, or its good work interfered with. As for myself, I will be halfway around the world by morning."

"Our dangerous friends will find you."

"Ah, yes. Those dangerous friends. Your dossier indicates that you're probably referring to Veil Kendry, whose martial-arts students have been guarding your brownstone for the past few months, and John 'Chant' Sinclair. If Mr. Kendry chooses to do anything but continue on with his very successful career as an artist, we'll kill him too. As for Mr. Sinclair, not even we know where he is these days, but it's safe to assume that self-employed mercenary is mounting yet another sting operation against us or our friends to steal our money. I doubt he has any idea what you're involved in, and if he does he probably doesn't care. No, it's only the two of you who remain as obstacles— but not for long."

"Why schlep us all the way back to New York to kill us?"

"I thought you understood. There is great power for me in killing you myself, in a particular manner, in this particular place. I will keep your hearts in a place of honor on my altar. I shall dispose of the rest of you."

"I'm touched."

He drew himself up, breathed deeply, exhaled slowly. Guy Fournier looked immensely pleased with himself. "Now, is there anything else on your mind you'd like to discuss while we wait for your brother to wake up? As you can see, I rather enjoy talking to you."

"I'll bet you say that to all your victims. You just love to hear yourself talk."

"I can assure you that you're the first to utter anything but screams, Frederickson. I'm enjoying studying your behavior under stress. You are a truly remarkable man. When I cut you, I won't be surprised if I draw ice water."

I pretended to ponder his invitation, then said, "I guess there's nothing left except to tell you I know your secret, and I know you're a liar. I know what's really going on here."

He looked genuinely puzzled, and he absently ran a bloodstained hand back through his thick, white hair. "What do you mean, I'm a liar?"

I nodded toward the bulge in the front of his robe. "All this chitchat and the anticipation of what you're eventually going to do excites you. That hard-on you've got tells me this whole business is more about sex than power, voodoo or otherwise. You're no voodoo master. Blow out your candles, and you're just a garden-variety necrophiliac who likes to dress up and who gets his rocks off by carving people up, or ordering them carved up. Do you eat your kills?"

He didn't like that at all. His dark eyes flashed with anger, and he took a step backward. I'd put Dr. Guy Fournier in high dudgeon. "I *am* a voodoo master!" he announced indignantly.

"Yeah, yeah, yeah. What you are is a corpse-fucker with a CIA day job. When you're not fucking stiffs, you're jerking off thinking about them. You may know a lot about Garth and me, but I also know a lot about people like you. I used to make a living writing papers and lecturing about people like you. Since you're going to kill us anyway, the least you can do is spare me all your voodoo bullshit. Probably everything else you've been telling me is bullshit too. Shadow Ops, indeed. You're just one more CIA flunky, probably a contract killer. Freaks like you are a dime a dozen. You're no different from Piggott; you may have known a little more, but the company still used both of you like Kleenex. You killed your flunkies when their usefulness was at an end, so don't be surprised if your masters dispose of *you* when all this is over."

Color rose on his high cheekbones. "You are wrong, Frederickson."

I heard Garth stir. I turned my head to the left, saw that he had regained consciousness. He had raised his head and was looking around. Our eyes met, and he said evenly, "I'm going to kill that damn horse."

My laughter was loud, long, and genuine. "Now, Garth, let's not blame our ill fortune on some dumb animal."

"I specifically asked the stable manager for a *nice* horse. You remember?"

"Your horse was very nice. You just didn't know how to ride her. But it's all worked out. Look who we've found."

"This creep is Fournier?"

"That's him."

"How come he's got a hard-on?"

"Actually, we were just discussing that phenomenon. He's a corpse-fucker, a necrophiliac. Think Jeffrey Dahmer with a Ph.D. in a high-rent district. Guy Fournier, I'd like to introduce you to my brother, Garth."

"A corpse-fucker," Garth said, clucking his tongue. "That's interesting. Listen, Mongo, whatever plan of escape you've developed, I hope it doesn't involve horses."

"No horses. The fact of the matter is that I've been waiting for you to wake up so that you can tell Fournier here to go fuck himself."

"Me? Why don't you do it?"

"I thought you should do it."

"We'll flip a coin."

"I always lose coin tosses with you. Actually, I've been trying to convince Guy that it would be in his best interests to surrender to us."

"Any luck?"

"The jury's still out. I suspect he's thinking about it. I mentioned the fact that, sooner or later, Veil or Chant Sinclair will feed him his balls if he kills us."

*"Be quiet!"* Fournier snapped, abruptly stepping forward into the narrow space between the two tables and glaring down at me. The nostrils in his aquiline nose flared, and his lips were compressed in a thin line. "I already caught this act of yours back in my office, Frederickson. You couldn't fool me again, even if you were in a position to capitalize on it."

"Damn. If you won't surrender, and I can't fool you, what am I supposed to do?"

"This seeming nonchalance in the face of death, this witty banter with your captors; it's described in your dossier. It's a game you play. You're trying to throw me off guard, trick me."

"Is it working?"

Fournier's response was to suddenly extend the knife toward my brother's face, holding the tip of the blade less than an inch from his right eyeball. A chill rippled through me, and I quickly looked away so that Fournier couldn't see the terror on my face. He said, "I think you'll find the situation less amusing when I start stabbing your brother's eyes out."

"You can make us scream, Fournier," I replied quickly, turning my head back to meet his gaze. "That's no big trick, and it's been done before. That doesn't make you a voodoo master. No matter what you do to us, you're still just a corpse-fucker with delusions of grandeur."

"Yeah," Garth said evenly, looking directly at the knife tip millimeters from his eyeball. "So go fuck yourself."

The Haitian's eyes rolled back up into his head. He turned toward Garth, wrapped both hands around the elongated handle of the knife and raised the blade over his head, directly above Garth's chest. Then he began to chant softly in Creole.

My heart pounding and my breath catching in my throat, I strained with all my strength at the leather strap around my right wrist. Blood flowed, ligaments stretched, joints creaked—and suddenly my right hand slipped free. But I'd run out of time.

*"Die!"* Fournier shouted in English, and went up on his toes to drive the knife into Garth's chest.

Incredibly, it looked like Mongo the Magnificent was going to slip from the jaws of death one more time, escaping even this second encounter with Guy Fournier, and indeed killing at least one of the people primarily responsible for Moby Dickens' death.

Mongo the Magnificent was not impressed.

The professor was in a killing frenzy, intoxicated with his voodoo rites and sexual pathology. It would only take me a few seconds to unbuckle the straps from my ankles and left wrist, and I was sure Guy Fournier was planning to dawdle much longer than that with the business of plunging the knife home into Garth's chest, and then carving out his heart. Fournier would be dead, his neck broken, long before he finished the job. But Garth would be dead too. Not that his sacrifice wouldn't have been worthwhile. If I survived, there was still a chance I could prevent the assassinations of the president and vice president and the hijacking of the country. With what I now knew and with Fournier's corpse in tow, along with any other evidence I might find in this place, it was even possible I could take it over the top and put lots of CIA people, if not their whole apparatus, out of business permanently. With both of us dead, however, Fournier and his CIA handlers would just keep on truckin', possibly for a very long time, in a fascist America under the stewardship of President William P. Kranes. Garth's loss of life would not only serve to save mine, but also, in all likelihood, that of the United States of America. The stakes were astronomical, and so using Garth's death to save myself, kill Fournier, and put an end to all the impending brand of insanity seemed the only sane thing to do.

But Mongo the Magnificent was still not moved by the logic of his thinking. Not long before, when I had been about to throw Moby Dickens out of my office, Garth had reminded me of the things that were meaningful, and I didn't need another reminder. I found that the prospect of survival, or of William P. Kranes becoming president, or the CIA prevailing, or the prospect of a fascist America, no longer interested me at all. What was important was that I hadn't had a chance to say good-bye to my brother.

"Hey, shithead!" I shouted, reaching across my body with my free hand, grabbing a fistful of yellow robe, and yanking hard just as Fournier started to plunge the knife downward. "You've got a loose dwarf back here!"

My yank had thrown Fournier off balance and thrown off his aim. The knife blade missed Garth and glanced off the edge of the marble tabletop. At least I had the satisfaction of giving the Haitian a good scare, because he must have jumped at least a foot in the air as he uttered a high-pitched sound that sounded like the yip of a small dog. When he came back down to earth he spun around, and his eyes went wide and his mouth dropped open when he saw me clawing frantically with my free right hand at the buckle of the strap on my left wrist. I ceased my token effort and lay back down on the cold marble when Fournier pressed the knife to my throat.

"Mongo!"

"Just wanted to say good-bye, Garth! I love you, and it's been a hell of a ride!"

*"Cut him and you die, sir! If that hand with the knife so much as twitches, I'll blow you in two!"*

Wooaa. My heart skipped a beat or three, squeezed by both astonishment and hope. I could feel warm blood trickling down my neck, but my throat wasn't slashed, because I was still breathing through my nose and mouth as opposed to spraying blood all over the ceiling. The pressure of the sharp steel on my flesh eased somewhat, and then the knife moved away a few inches to where I could see it. I turned slightly, craned my neck a little to look behind me to where the voice had come from, and saw . . . Francisco. He looked very pale, but his hands were steady. The shiny, new double-barreled shotgun he was aiming at Guy Fournier's chest still had the price tag dangling from the trigger guard.

"Francisco!" I said, giggling hysterically. "I hope you don't think that working late like this means I'm going to pay you overtime!"

"You promoted me to associate investigator, sir. I assumed that meant I was no longer working on the clock, so I couldn't qualify for overtime any more."

Garth said, "Mongo, you promoted this employee to associate investigator without consulting me?"

"Hey, I'm the senior partner, remember? Besides, the promotion was only temporary."

"Well, I suggest we make the promotion permanent."

"Agreed. Francisco, your promotion to associate investigator is now officially permanent."

"Thank you, sir."

"You're welcome. You've earned it. Now shoot this son of a bitch, will you?"

Fournier, who'd suffered his second severe shock in less than a minute, didn't seem to know quite what to make of our business discussion, although he was clearly not amused by it. Still, the expression on his triangular face was almost comical. He kept blinking very rapidly, as if in disbelief, and his thin lips were again pressed together so tightly that white, bloodless lines had appeared at the corners of his mouth. His bright, expressive eyes swam with both rage and confusion as he abruptly pressed the blade back against my jugular and moved closer to me to where he was almost lying across my chest. "Drop that gun, Francisco," he said, his deep voice quavering ever so slightly. "If you don't, this man dies right now. I'll slice his head right off."

"Then you'll die too. I'll give you both barrels right in the gut."

Francisco's tone was perfectly even, steadier than Fournier's. I was impressed. I said, "Just shoot him, Francisco."

"I can't do that without risk of hitting you, sir. The shells are loaded with buckshot. I don't know much about guns, and I didn't want to take a chance on missing the target if I did have to shoot."

"If you'll pardon the expression, Francisco, I can live with that risk. He won't back off because he has everything to lose, and we can't hang around here all night. That's what he wants. He knows that the longer you stand there holding that big gun, the heavier it's going to start to feel. The muscles in your hands and arms will begin to cramp. He figures that sooner or later you'll lose your aim or drop your guard. Then he'll slit my throat and try to duck away behind the tables. So drop the bastard now while you've got the chance, before your muscles start to get sore. I'm your boss, and I'm ordering you to stop worrying about me and pull the fucking trigger."

"Belay that order, Francisco," my brother said quietly.

"You didn't have to tell me that, Garth," Francisco said dryly. "Now that I'm a permanent associate investigator, I have to make critical decisions like that myself."

I watched Fournier's Adam's apple bob up and down. "He's as insane as the two of you," he said in a strained whisper.

I grunted. "Must be something in the air at the brownstone."

"He makes clever remarks when you're about to die!"

"No, he makes clever remarks when you're about to die."

The pressure of the knife blade against my throat increased ever so slightly. "Make him put the gun down, Frederickson," he whispered hoarsely, his mouth close to my ear. "Otherwise, I'll slaughter you like a pig. If he does put the gun down, I'll leave here without hurting you."

"Go fuck yourself, Professor. First of all, you lie, and even if you weren't a liar I don't want you going anywhere. You're the voodoo master; you make him put the gun down. Cast a spell on him. If you were really a voodoo master instead of a weirdo who jerks off thinking about dead bodies, that's what you'd do. Go on, Fournier; voodoo him."

Fournier lifted his head away from my chest and stared down at me. Strange shadows moved in his midnight eyes, and his expression changed. I couldn't tell what he was thinking, but the razor edge of the knife blade remained pressed snugly against my carotid artery.

"Be careful, shithead," Garth said, chuckling. "Watch out for my brother. I'm telling you he's a silver-tongued devil. He can talk people into anything, and right now he's trying to talk you into getting yourself killed."

"Shit, Garth," I said. "There you go again, letting the cat out of the bag. You take all the fun out of things."

"I just like to see you fight fair, Mongo. You're the only sorcerer in this room, but this shithead doesn't realize it. I just thought he should be given fair warning of who he's up against."

"You're such a spoilsport."

"Fournier, I'm warning you that you'd better think twice before you do anything my brother suggests, because, even strapped to that table, he has more personal power and will than you've ever had, or will have. All you've got is a knife, a hard-on, and a line of bullshit. Let him into your head, and you're a goner."

"Spoilsport, spoilsport."

"So let's stop fucking around here, Fournier. As things now stand, two of us are going to die here tonight—Mongo, when you think the time is right and you suddenly cut his throat, and you when Francisco shows you what a mistake you've made and blows a hole through your chest. That will leave just Francisco and me to put an end to this assassination business and then spread the word that Dr.

Guy Fournier, renowned hero to millions of Haitians, was never more than a flunky murderer for the CIA and a corpse-fucker, and really stupid to boot. There's no point in killing my brother, because it means instant death for you. What's the point? Give it up. You'd have saved yourself all this extra aggravation if you'd just followed my brother's suggestion in the first place and surrendered. Like Mongo said, we'll see that you're safely tucked away somewhere. Just think of how much fun you'll have testifying before Congress and curling the toes of all those pompous, chickenshit politicians."

Somewhat to my surprise, the Haitian appeared to be giving it some thought. "It's too late to stop the assassinations," he said at last in a throaty whisper. "There won't be any congressional committees to testify to. They'll kill me."

I cleared my throat. "Oh, don't be such a pessimist, Professor. I think Garth has made some excellent points. The president and vice president may already be dead, but don't forget that William P. Kranes isn't going to remain in office very long once Garth and Francisco leave here and the whole story comes out. Maybe I won't talk you into killing yourself after all. Why don't we all just walk out of here together, and Garth and I will introduce you to some of our FBI acquaintances. Garth's right; they'll fall all over themselves when they hear the dirt you have to dish on the CIA. And we promise not to tell anyone you're just a silly old corpse-fucker. What do you say? Ollie Ollie in come free?"

He didn't have anything to say, at least not for some time. Finally he leaned close once again and whispered in my ear, "You and your brother make fun of me. You don't think it can be done, do you?"

"Uh . . . I don't think what can be done?"

Fournier, still keeping the knife blade pressed to my throat, straightened up and turned toward Francisco. "You're Roman Catholic, aren't you?"

"Yes," Francisco replied evenly.

Fournier very slowly reached across my body with his free hand, pressed my right arm back down on the marble, closed the leather strap around my bleeding wrist, and buckled it tightly. "Do you know that I'm a Roman Catholic priest, Francisco?" His voice was once again confident and steady, low and soothing.

"You were a priest. I don't think the Holy Father would approve of your activities."

"Once a priest, my son, always a priest. No matter what your reason, kill me and you'll burn forever in the fires of hell. You'll have committed a mortal sin in killing me, a sin made even more grievous by the fact that the man you murdered was a priest. There can be no forgiveness."

Incredibly, Guy Fournier—prodded by Garth's masterful, if off-the-wall, goading—seemed to be taking up my challenge to persuade Francisco to put down the shotgun.

"Watch out, Francisco," I said through clenched teeth, drawing in my chin as far as I could in an effort to ease the pressure of the knife blade on my carotid artery. "He's making a run at your head."

"I'm aware of that, sir."

"Shoot him, don't talk to him."

"Not yet, Francisco," Garth said softly. "He's still too close to Mongo."

"I know, Garth."

"Do you want to burn in hell, Francisco?"

"You're to drop the knife, release those restraints, and then move away from the tables. Then nobody has to die."

"You're also homosexual, aren't you?"

Francisco did not reply.

"That, too, is a mortal sin. But I can forgive you, Francisco. I can give you grace."

"I don't need your forgiveness, Mr. Fournier. My parish priest is homosexual."

"Which of these men do you love, Francisco?"

"Both of them, but not in the way you mean." Our new permanent associate investigator paused, then added wryly, "They're not my type."

"Sexually, you mean. Am I your type?"

"Are you propositioning me, Mr. Fournier?"

"I'm offering you the best sex you've ever had, Francisco, but also so much more than that." He paused, used his free hand to slowly raise his robe to expose his priapic condition, then continued, "I offer you forgiveness."

I said, "That's very droll, shithead. You call your dong 'Forgiveness'?"

He ignored me. He continued to stare hypnotically at Francisco, speaking in a tone that was reassuring and sensual. "I can give you orgasms, Francisco, but I also offer you more power and money than you can imagine. You can travel the world with me, and never have to worry about any physical, emotional, or sexual need ever again. The organization I'm part of will provide you with everything. I think you realize how powerful we are, because you've been helping your employers try to expose just a small part of our activities. Do you believe that I'm telling you the truth?"

"I'm aware that you work for a very powerful organization," Francisco replied in a flat tone.

"Good. I'm asking you to join me in that organization, be at my side. The price is betrayal of these men you love, but that's nothing compared to what you will gain. Betrayal is not only the price of power, but the very essence of power itself. I will replace them. You will love me, as I will love you. Just think about it for a moment. Think of what I am offering you. Help these men now, and they will only become more rich and famous—while your life will remain the same. Help me, and wealth and power will be yours."

Francisco said nothing.

"Francisco . . . ?"

"You have to be more specific, Mr. Fournier. I believe you can provide me with these things, but how do I know you will? How do I know I can trust you?"

Fournier abruptly dropped the hem of his robe, then glanced down at me. There was a smirk on his face and a gleam of triumph in his eyes. He took the knife away from my throat and dropped it on the floor, where it landed with a loud, metallic clatter. "I've dropped my knife, Francisco," he said softly. "Now you lower your shotgun. I will show you that you can trust me. I want to hold you in my arms, have you hold me. I will do things to you. Then you'll know."

Fournier moved out of my line of sight, his bare feet padding on the floor as he walked toward Francisco. I counted six steps before the deafening roar of both barrels of the shotgun being fired boomed in the chamber. Pieces of Guy Fournier splattered over me, and I screwed my eyes shut and spat. When I opened my eyes again I found an ashen-faced Francisco beside me reaching out with trembling hands to unfasten the leather strap buckled around my left wrist.

"I may be Roman Catholic and homosexual," he said in a low voice that now quavered with shock, "but I'm not stupid."

"Nicely done, Francisco," Garth said. "*Very* nicely done."

When my wrists were free, I sat up and began unbuckling the straps around my ankles as Francisco turned and started to attend to Garth. I asked, "How the hell did you find this place?"

"Information about it was on the computer diskette, sir. It was one of the first things the Slurper found and decrypted. Fournier kept an online diary, along with records of everything he did here—dates, names of victims, even photographs. He paid his rent and utility bills

electronically, so there was an address listed, along with the combination to the electronic lock on the main entrance. Now I think he
must have kept the diary and pictures for sexual purposes." He
gagged slightly, turned his face away. "My God, I've murdered a
man."

"It's called pest control, Francisco," I said, swinging my legs over
the side of the table and rubbing my wrists and ankles as Garth, now
free, did the same. "It's also called self-defense. A man like Fournier
knows lots of ways to kill a man, and, if you hadn't shot him, he'd
have broken your neck the second he was close enough to get his
hands on you. Besides, he was threatening you with a knife."

"But he'd dropped the knife, sir. I shot him in cold blood."

"My blood was hot enough for both of us. Besides, I didn't see him
drop the knife. Did you see him drop the knife, Garth?"

"I certainly did not," my brother replied in a firm tone. "You have
to get used to being a hero, Francisco. How'd you know we were
here?"

"I didn't. It was the only place I had to look."

"The last time we spoke, Mongo and I were on our way to Idaho."

"But you didn't check in like you were supposed to. The protocol,
remember?"

"We were always forgetting to check in."

"This time was different. You were supposed to check in within
forty-eight hours, and almost twice that much time had passed. I just
knew you were in terrible trouble. I felt sick. I didn't know what to
do. Then the Slurper decoded the diary and the references to this
place in it, and I thought maybe you'd been brought here. I had to do
something, and coming here was the only thing I could think of. I
bought the shotgun and shells on the way."

"Bless you, child," Garth said, abruptly grabbing Francisco under
the armpits, lifting him up off the floor and planting a loud, wet kiss

on his forehead. "Mongo, I think our new permanent associate investigator has already earned a raise."

"I think he deserves profit-sharing."

"Agreed."

"Thank you," a thoroughly embarrassed Francisco said as Garth set him back down on the floor.

I said, "Speaking of protocol, Francisco, why didn't you call Veil? That was the first thing you were supposed to do if you thought we might be in trouble."

"Veil wasn't home. I couldn't wait; I had to get here as soon as possible."

"And not a half second too soon. What about the police?"

"I did call the police. They didn't take your disappearance seriously; they said the two of you were disappearing all the time, and the only people I should be worrying about were whoever you'd disappeared with. They said they were going to send a detective around to look at the photographs from Fournier's computer files, and then consider getting a search warrant for this place, but I couldn't wait for all that to happen."

"You do nice work, Francisco. Thank you."

"Thank you, sir."

"All right," I said to Garth as I hopped down off the table to the floor, "rest time is over. Fournier said the president and vice president were probably already dead, but that doesn't make it so. We've got to find our clothes and a phone, not necessarily in that order."

# CHAPTER 14

We found neither, but behind one of the two doors at the far end of the loft we did find a toilet and laundry sink, where Garth and I washed Fournier's blood off us as best we could. Behind the second door was a small storeroom filled with voodoo paraphernalia and a pipe rack with a half-dozen robes similar to the one Fournier had been wearing.

"Here," Garth said, tossing me one of the robes. "This will have to do."

Garth was about the dead Haitian's height, so his robe fit just fine. Mine did not, to say the least; I looked like a neon, voodoo version of Casper the Ghost. I ended up wrapping it around my body like a sarong, and then we quickly followed Francisco out of the ceremonial chamber toward the front, through narrow corridors and past storage rooms filled with what appeared to be old theatrical props and dilapidated sets. We emerged in a small parking lot of a warehouse abutting Twelfth Avenue. The first thing I took note of was the relative quiet.

"It hasn't gone down yet," Garth said, echoing my thoughts. "If it had, all hell would be breaking loose—helicopters, ambulances, and police cars all over the place."

"Right," I said, looking around me. "Now all we have to do is find a way to stop it."

We were only a few blocks away from the convention center, and traffic was sparse as canny New Yorkers took alternate routes around the cavernous building to avoid the inevitable road blocks and potential traffic jams. There were no cabs, which was a moot point since it was unlikely any hack driver would pick up a party of three with two of them dressed like Garth and me. There were also no pay phones in sight. There were buildings, presumably with phones, on either side of us, what looked to be production studios for various television shows being shot in the city, but they were sealed off by high chain-link fences topped with coils of razor wire.

My pulse quickened when I suddenly heard the sound of sirens approaching from the north. My first thought was that it was a convoy of ambulances speeding to the site of a double assassination, but the sirens turned out to belong to a brigade of police on motorcycles escorting a stretch limousine with smoked windows that streaked by.

Garth said, "Somebody must be late."

"Over here, sir!" Francisco shouted from where he had wandered off to the side of the building, where there was a narrow alleyway. "There's a car!"

Garth and I sprinted to the alleyway, saw a dark green Ford Taurus parked a few yards away, next to a side exit. The car doors were unlocked, and the key was in the ignition. Garth climbed in behind the wheel, I got in beside him, and Francisco jumped in the back. Garth started the car and, with the tires squealing, first backed out of the alleyway, then turned the car and tore out onto Twelfth Avenue, the rear end of the car fishtailing as we headed for the Jacob Javits Convention Center.

We'd gone barely a third of a mile when we turned a corner and came to a road block set up to detour traffic east, around the convention center. Garth and I knew the patrol officer leaning idly against one of the yellow barricades, a cop by the name of Harriet Boone. She started when she saw our car barreling down Eleventh Avenue toward the barricades. She jumped out into the road and began frantically waving her arms, then jumped back when Garth braked the car to a sliding, screeching halt next to her cruiser. She started to reach for her gun, then froze and gaped as Francisco, my voodoo-robed brother, and I leaped out of the car.

"Mongo?! Garth?! What the hell are you—"

"Harriet, there isn't time to explain why we're dressed like this," I said quickly. "Every second counts. You have to get on your radio right now and say anything you have to in order to get word to the Secret Service that they must keep the president and vice president off the stage, or get them off *immediately* if that's where they are now. There are two assassins down in the front rows getting ready to pop them. Then get us into the hall. We can identify the shooters."

The woman, who still seemed stunned, shook her head in disbelief. "Mongo, there's no way I can get you in there. Security is even tighter than usual. There have been reports that somebody is planning to try to kill the president."

"Harriet," I said, grimacing with frustration, "you're not listening to me. Garth and I are responsible for those reports and the tightened security. But it's not going to do any good unless we act now. The shooters are already in the hall, probably sitting with some delegation that's close to the stage. Both the president and vice president are going to *die* unless you do what I ask."

A big, strong hand gripped my right shoulder, turned me around. I found myself looking up at a very solidly built man wearing a dark suit, sunglasses, a plug in his ear, and a Secret Service pin in his lapel. His right hand was inside his suit jacket, and he was leaning back slightly on his heels. "What's this talk about assassination?" he asked curtly.

"Look, you're just the man I want—"

"I heard what you said. I want to see identification from the three of you."

I flipped the ends of my robe in exasperation. "I seem to have left my wallet home."

Harriet said, "I can vouch for these men."

The Secret Service agent was unimpressed. "I don't care who you vouch for, Officer. We've got three men here who drive up in a speeding car, two of them dressed in clown suits, and one of them talking about assassination. Now, I want the three of you to turn around slowly and put your hands on top of the car."

"You're a fucking idiot," Garth said as he stepped forward and hit the man with a snake-quick jab to the point of the chin. The man's knees buckled and he went down.

"My God," Harriet murmured, staring in horror at the unconscious man lying on the pavement at her feet. "You can't hit a Secret Service agent."

Garth went to the police cruiser, opened the door on the driver's side. "Harriet, you've got two choices; shoot us, or get us down the block to that hall. Otherwise, we're just going to take your car."

"You stay here!" I shouted to Francisco as I opened the rear door of the cruiser and jumped in.

"No, sir," Francisco replied evenly as he clambered into the car beside me. With impeccable logic, he added, "You couldn't have gotten this far without me. I'm going with the two of you."

"Harriet?" Garth said calmly. "Hurry up and make up your mind what you're going to do."

"Garth, this could cost me my pension!"

"Or get you a medal and a promotion."

"You're going to get yourselves killed if you try to barge in there!"

"We're counting on you and your police radio to keep that from happening. Come on, Harriet. This is righteous. You're about to help prevent two assassinations."

Now the woman reacted, brushing past Garth and sliding in behind the wheel. Garth raced around to the other side of the car and got in beside her.

"This is Officer Boone with a Code Fury emergency!" the policewoman shouted into her microphone as she started up the cruiser, floored the accelerator, and crashed through the wooden barriers in front of her. "Somebody's getting ready to shoot the president and vice president! Get them to safety *now!* I'm bringing in three men who can identify the assassins! Hold your fire!"

Within less than thirty seconds we had reached the convention center. Harriet braked to a skidding halt beside the stretch limousine that had passed us earlier, and which was now parked up on the sidewalk near an entrance where the door had been left open. Garth, Francisco, and I jumped out of the car. Harriet started to follow, but I pushed her back behind the wheel. "Stay on the radio, Harriet! Keep broadcasting that message!"

A policeman was just coming to close the door when the three of us came barreling through, with Garth pushing the man aside and over a steel railing. Ten yards in front of us was another policeman manning a metal detector, and beyond him a spacious lobby with a stone floor. Three large television monitors suspended from the ceiling broadcast pictures and sound of what was taking place inside the enormous hall on the other side of the closed doors where we were headed; the president and vice president, flanked by their families and a gaggle of politicians, were standing inches from the edge of the stage, holding each other's hands aloft as they accepted the thunderous cheers and applause of the hundreds of delegates in the hall who had risen to their feet.

Garth and I hadn't had time to discuss just what we were going to do if and when we did get this far, but we both seemed to have the same idea in mind. At that very moment the two assassins could be tensing, getting ready to remove the plastic guns mounted under their chairs, step out into the aisle or into the well before the stage for a clear shot, aim, and fire at their exposed targets. There was no time to stop and try to reason with anybody. We had to make it through the double doors on the other side of the lobby; one glimpse of Garth and me in our voodoo robes bursting into the auditorium, shouting and waving our arms, would be enough to get the president and vice president buried under a lifesaving avalanche of Secret Service agents.

We sprinted through the metal detector, past the startled policeman who had leaped out of his chair and was reaching for his gun. I heard a collision of bodies behind me, and when I glanced back over my shoulder I could see that Francisco, bless his quick-thinking and courageous permanent-associate-investigator's heart, had hurled himself through the air and into the man in order to save us from being shot in the back.

His effort was for naught. I had only glanced back for a split second, but when I looked ahead again I saw that five men, three of them large enough to play on the San Diego Chargers' line, had materialized between us and the double doors. They were all in a crouched firing stance. One had his gun aimed at Francisco, and the other four had a direct bead on Garth and me.

*"Freeze!"* the man in the middle of the pack shouted, his voice cutting like a chainsaw through the cacophonous clapping and cheering coming from the television speaker hanging above his head.

Garth and I, the bottoms of our bare feet coated with gravel, slid to a halt and raised our hands. I shouted back, "Listen to us!"

"Shut up! Don't talk!"

"Get the president and vice president off the stage right now," I said loudly but calmly, carefully enunciating each word. "They're about to be shot."

"I said don't talk! Lie down on your stomachs with your arms out to the sides! Do it right now, or you're dead men!"

Garth and I glanced at each other, and once again I could see that we were thinking the same thing. With our reports and warnings we had created quite a fuss over the past few days, and there was enormous tension. As disciplined as these Secret Service agents were, their trigger fingers had to be getting a bit itchy, and I didn't much care for the irony of Garth and me dying as a direct result of the very alertness and caution we had labored so hard to bring about. If we were a few yards short of the goal line, there was nothing to be done about it, except do what we were told or risk being gunned down. We lay down on our stomachs, spread our arms out to the sides.

Instantly four of the men sprang forward, while the fifth rushed over to Francisco. Guns were held to the backs of our heads while our hands were roughly pulled behind our backs and our wrists cuffed. I could hear the cuffs being snapped on Francisco's wrists, and I was very conscious of the smell of industrial-strength wax on the cold stone where my cheek rested.

Something had changed besides our situation; something was different, and with my thoughts racing and heart pounding it took me a few moments to realize what it was.

The applause and cheering had stopped; there was dead silence from behind the doors and over the television monitors.

Then a voice, very faint but still audible, could be heard over the television speaker. The voice said, *"Don't do it."*

The voice, as muted as it was, sounded familiar. Suddenly the hands that had been holding my head to the marble lifted. Five Secret Service agents and their three captives all looked up at the television monitors, transfixed. And I now realized who had been in the limousine that had passed us on Twelfth Avenue.

It appeared that being Speaker of the House of Representatives was good enough to get you not only a police escort through New York City, but into the convention of the opposing party, and even onto the convention floor itself. It also appeared that William P. Kranes had taken my advice and bellied up to the bar with some of his loonier right-wing admirers. Somebody had given him an earful, and he obviously hadn't liked what he'd heard. Perhaps for the first time the full import of what Garth and I had been trying to tell him had finally sunk in, and he wanted no part, however passively, of any assassination plot. He did not want to preside over the corpse of a country.

The camera picked him up, and then zoomed in on the pudgy man as he slowly walked down the center of the carpeted well separating the stage from the convention delegates. He didn't know where to look, and so he was looking everywhere, out across the sea of faces, alternately waving his arms and then making thrusting motions with his palms out, as if to push back the death he knew was lurking in the hall.

*"Don't do it,"* he repeated, his voice being barely picked up by the microphone on stage. His voice sounded like it was coming from the far end of a long tunnel. The camera moved back to include the stage, where everybody except a dozen scurrying Secret Service agents was staring at Kranes in stunned amazement. *"This isn't the way. It won't do you any good. I won't be president. I don't want to be president. I've resigned as Speaker of the House, so it isn't—"*

Suddenly there was a blur of motion and sound. Secret Service agents had already surrounded the president and vice president, but still two young men whom I immediately recognized as the assassins appeared on the apron of the well, holding their guns aloft, searching for their targets. An instant before they were shot dead by Secret Service agents, the head of William P. Kranes exploded in an expanding mist of blood, flesh, and bone that sprayed the faces of the people on the stage and in the front rows of the screaming delegates.

The screams and shouts increased in volume as the pandemonium breaking loose could clearly be heard through the heavy doors as well as over the television speakers.

"Hey, big guy," Garth said to the burly agent standing over him and gaping at the television monitor. "You want to cut us loose now? It looks like you've got other business to attend to."

# EPILOGUE

*M*y God," *Mary Tree said, lifting her head off Garth's* shoulder and looking over at me. "Harper and I can't leave you two alone for more than a day, can we? Garth almost breaks his neck falling off a *horse,* of all things, and then both of you wind up almost getting your hearts cut out in some voodoo temple!"

Almost was, of course, the delicious operative word. Other good news was that I hadn't drooled, awake or asleep, for almost a week, and my headache had finally disappeared after the fourth day. I took these as hopeful signs that Mongo the Magnificent was not going to end as Robby the Zombie. In fact, all things considered, I was feeling pretty good.

Garth's wife, the folksinger Mary Tree, had canceled three concerts in Norway and Sweden to fly back to New York when news of what had happened, and the Fredericksons' involvement in events, had hit the news services around the world. And Harper Rhys-Whitney, who was now officially my fiancée, had returned from her latest snake-hunting expedition in the Amazon rain forest and was sitting at my side on the sofa in my apartment. Garth and Mary lounged in easy chairs across from us, and Francisco and his lover, Tony, sat in straight-backed chairs on either side of them. Tony, Francisco's "type," turned out to be a wiry, very soft-spoken principal dancer with the New York City Ballet. We had invited Francisco to bring Tony and join us for drinks before we went our separate ways— Garth and Mary back to Europe to resume her tour, and Harper and I off to Tahiti. The dancer kept glancing shyly and admiringly at Francisco, who appeared very pleased with himself.

"Robby," Harper said seriously, reaching over and squeezing my hand, "do you really think it was the CIA that killed Kranes?"

I gazed into Harper's impossibly maroon eyes, then glanced at Garth, who grunted and rolled his eyes toward the ceiling. He said, "You can bet your pet python and the snake farm on it, Harper."

"Dr. Frederickson—"

"Don't call me 'Dr. Frederickson,' Tony. And don't call me 'Robert' or 'Robby,' because only my mother and Harper do that, probably because they know I hate it, and only Francisco can't seem to escape the need to call me 'sir.' My name's Mongo."

"Mongo," the dancer said, "there's something I don't understand. If those people in the CIA already had two assassins on the convention floor, why put a third sniper up in the ceiling beams?"

I shrugged. "We'll probably never know for certain, because the sniper, not surprisingly, wasn't caught, and it isn't very likely that the responsible parties will be forthcoming. But there seem to be two possibilities. The first is that they planned all along to have a sniper up there as backup just in case their Right-to-Life patsies got cold feet or missed. The killings could still be blamed on them and their radical associates, since they would be caught with guns on the convention floor. Then the shooter opted to kill Kranes when Kranes suddenly appeared on the convention floor, and it looked like the jig was up and they were going to be exposed. Kranes was killed to cover their tracks, so he couldn't testify about who he'd talked to, and what he'd heard that caused him to come to New York and the convention in the first place."

Garth explained the second possibility. "Or the sniper was sent in at the last moment specifically to kill Kranes in the event he did what he did. They had time. Kranes announced his resignation in Washington before hopping on the shuttle to New York. The CIA knew their former choice for president could suddenly end up causing them big-time trouble. He was a man who could single-handedly destroy the entire agency if he took a mind to it."

Tony frowned. "But how could they get a man armed with a rifle and silencer into the hall past the kind of security they had there?"

I laughed. "Tony, there are some things the CIA does very well. Remember that they managed to place two shooters in a state delegation with front-row seats, didn't they?"

Mary ran a hand back through her waist-length, silver-streaked blond hair and fixed me with her sea blue eyes. "Mongo, what's going to happen now?"

I smiled. "You and Garth are flying off to Europe, and Harper and I are going to Tahiti."

"Stop it! You know what I mean. What's going to happen?"

"The truth?"

"Of course."

Garth said, "Nothing's going to happen. All the people we know of who had any connection to the conspiracy are dead—including Taylor Mackintosh, who the paper says got drunk and fell off the balcony of his twentieth-floor apartment in Trump Tower. Cowboys one, Indians zero—as usual. We lost this one."

There were a few moments of silence, and then Harper asked, "Is it true, Mongo? The CIA is going to get away with this and the agency will stay the same?"

"I'm not quite as much a pessimist as my brother," I replied, wincing slightly, "but I'm afraid he's probably right. It depends on how far out of the sky the American eagle has fallen, and the old bird has been looking a little sickly. Americans have always been good at denial, and the country's politics of late have only made them better at it."

"But the commission's report will be out, and everything that's happened to the two of you will be in it."

"Sure," I said, and shrugged. "But, outside of the company's money-laundering operations in Haiti, we can't prove anything. That means our discussion of the murders of the two justices and the conspiracy to assassinate the president and vice president will be anecdotal, included in an appendix so that it won't taint the hard data we do have. The report won't be out for months, and by then we'll almost certainly have a right-wing president who's unlikely to act on most of the recommendations the commission will probably make. The CIA and right-wing politicians are already mounting a counterattack, claiming the company had nothing to do with any of this. They're also cobbling together a story that the attempted assassinations were part of a left-wing conspiracy to discredit conservative causes and destroy the CIA. That's all you'll be hearing on talk radio."

Francisco snorted angrily—probably the most emotion I'd ever seen the man display. "How can they claim that when two of their assassins were antiabortion fanatics?"

"It's easy," Garth replied. "They just claim it—and keep on claiming it. They'll say the Right-to-Life shooters were dupes. Like Mongo says, all you're going to be hearing on talk radio and reading in the right-wing press for months is how this was all part of a radical left-wing conspiracy. By the time the report is actually published, most of what's in it will have been leaked, considered old hat, and probably discredited by a majority of Americans. How could people have believed all the things that got us the crop of no-brain right-wing politicians we have in office now? People believe what they want to believe, Francisco, and they're not going to want to believe you, Mongo, and me. Right now Americans want a kind of chicken-fried, good-old-boy fascist government that's safe for business and the wealthy and dangerous to women and children. That's the bad news. The good news is that we don't give a shit. Right, Mongo?"

I smiled thinly. "Right."

Mary looked at her husband, said, "I don't believe neither of you care what happens to this country. You two are the most *American* Americans I've ever met."

Garth merely shrugged.

It was a lovely compliment, even if it wasn't entirely true. Garth had once been thoroughly *American,* in the sense that Mary meant, but his poisoning had changed a lot of things in him, opened up spooky depths in his soul I still did not think his wife fully understood, and it was probably just as well. I considered Garth more Intergalactic than American. As for myself, I had always *felt* intensely *American,* but in recent years it had begun to occur to me that the America I felt so much a part of was actually a myth. It had always been just a dream, and for too many people a nightmare, with some other, less magisterial, bird masquerading as an eagle. Vietnam had destroyed the illusion. I could have remarked that Garth and I had acted as we had for our own very personal reasons, with the murder of Moby Dickens at the top of the list and patriotism at the bottom, but I didn't. I didn't want to spoil the moment, or the compliment.

Harper put her hand on my knee—her touch instantly making me wish we were already in Tahiti, or anyplace else, for that matter, where we were alone. "Robby, what about Guy Fournier? Was he really part of some secret, secret organization in the CIA?"

"That's another thing I don't think we'll ever know for certain one way or another. The Operations Directorate is secretive to begin with, a world within itself. I suppose some kind of 'Shadow Ops' within Ops is a possibility, but I personally think he was bullshitting us. He was a man who loved to talk—a good thing, that, or otherwise Garth and I would be dead. A lot of psychopaths and sociopaths are like that—megalomaniacs who construct whole fantasy worlds to rule over. The fact is that Ops uses people like that all the time, and in reality he was probably a flunky only a little higher up the ladder than Paul Piggott."

"You're wrong, Mongo," Garth said simply. "He was telling the truth."

"There you go. What he told us is in our report. Congress can make up its own mind about whether or not they want to look into it."

Garth glanced at his watch, put down his drink, and got up from his chair. "Time to hit fthe road, folks. The limo should be downstairs."

We all rose. Francisco cleared his throat. "Uh, Garth? Sir? Do you really mean what you said before? I should keep the office open and run it myself while you're away?"

"Frederickson and Frederickson is all yours," Garth replied. "One of us will touch base with you from time to time, but for the most part you can decide what to commit us to—matters involving, say, murder or pillage. But absolutely no cases involving plagiarism. Those will have to wait until Mongo and I get back."

Francisco smiled. "Understood."

I said, "You're working on a profit-sharing basis now, Francisco, so make us some profits. Garth and I have been otherwise engaged for almost six months now, so the phones are likely to be pretty quiet. Tomorrow you might want to start touching base with all our regular corporate clients and see if you can't drum up some new business."

"I'll do that, sir. I appreciate your confidence."

As we trooped down the stairs together, in pairs, I heard Tony whisper to Francisco, "I want you to tell me again about what happened in the voodoo temple."

Garth muttered, "I'm still going to kill that damn horse."